I0778372

★★★★★ "This is a fun twist on the passion and practicality of Sense and Sensibility!" - Michelle, Goodreads

★★★★★ "I was completely captivated by these characters and got all the feels. Low angst but completely captivating. I loved this book - it was different than I expected but amazing all the same. I can't wait for more from Emma Lee Jayne and from this series!" - J, Goodreads

★★★★★ "This was a fantastic grumpy sunshine romance." - Sarah, Goodreads

★★★★★ "Great writing, a fun storyline, and a sweet happily ever after!"- Michelle, Goodreads

★★★★★ "What's better than a book you already know you will read again? In the last couple years I have become quite smitten with this author ... They are smart, quirky and sexy." - Ellabythesea, Amazon

★★★★★ "This was an amazing story!" - Kitty Libre, Amazon

sense & irritability

A GRUMPY-SUNSHINE, BOSS-EMPLOYEE, AUSTEN-INSPIRED ROMCOM

AUSTEN IN AUSTIN

EMMA LEE JAYNE

Sense & Irritability

Emma Lee Jayne

Edited by: Kat Baxter

Copyeditors: BookReadingJenn and Word Summit Editing

Book cover art: Mira Anders

With regard to digital publication, be advised that any alteration of font size or spacing by the reader could change the author's original format.

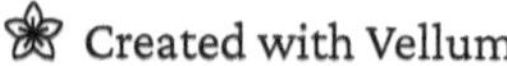 Created with Vellum

First off, a quick content warning:

This book deals with the (off-page) death of a parent.

Secondly, the hero of the book is neurodivergent, as many of my characters are. I occasionally get a review suggesting I write neurodiverse characters because it's trendy. I promise you this is not the case. My own family is chock full of neurodiversity, from my dad who is almost certainly on the spectrum, to my daughter who is as well, to my own rampant ADHD.

Also, since I've already come clean about my ADHD ... did you know that having a ton of typos is part of the diagnosis? Yes, I hire copyeditors. Two of them, in fact. But there are probably still some of those buggers in there. If you find a typo, please

reach out to me so I squash it like a bug!
Cheers!

Emma

*For the many readers who love my Emma Lee Jayne
books.
Thank you for trusting me with your precious free time.*

sense & irritability

one

SAVANNAH

"Can we both just agree that taking this job is a horrible idea?" my sister, Trinity, asks.

Her voice is coming from my bra because my ancient Corolla doesn't have a Bluetooth connection. So, if I want to obey Austin's hands-free driving laws, I have to shove my phone into my bra while I drive.

I'm out near the small town of Honey Lake, well outside the city limits, so theoretically there should be less traffic. Still, safe driving is safe driving.

"No," I tell Trinity. "You think it's a bad idea. I think it's my last, best hope of salvaging my career and staving off debtors' prison."

"You read too many historical romance novels. There are no debtors' prisons anymore."

Trinity, who is working on her PhD in psychology, is the smart one in the family, so she's probably right on both counts. "Okay then, it's my last, best hope of salvaging my career and staving off bankruptcy."

There's a beat of silence, and then Trinity asks, "Is it really that bad?"

Yes. However bad she's imagining, it's that bad. Or worse. My bank account is down to pennies and my credit cards are beyond maxed out. I still have bills rolling in from the law firm. And the worst—the absolute worst part, the part that keeps me up at night—is that I borrowed money from Mom. It was months ago, back when the lawyers assured me the case was a slam dunk.

I can't believe I fell for that shit.

I can't believe that—at twenty-six—I was stupid enough to let my mother take money out of her 401K. That was back when I was sure I would win. When I thought it was just a small probate issue.

Fuck. I was such a fool.

Here I am, a year later, drowning in debt, guilt, lies, and buried rage. And exhaustion.

God, I'm so tired of fighting everything. I'm so tired of losing.

Unfortunately, I take too long to respond to Trinity's question.

"If it's really that bad—" Her voice is uncharacteristically soft. "—You should let me help."

"Trin, you're in grad school. Aren't you barely living above the poverty line?"

"I could—"

"Absolutely not." There's no fucking way. I'm not dragging another family member down into this pit.

"I want to help." She sounds stung. "And I don't want you to do … this. This is madness."

I snort. "Stop being so dramatic. Being a personal chef is a real job. Lots of people do it."

"That's not the part that has me freaked out. It's all the … other stuff."

Her tone implies the "other stuff" is weird and kinky. Lurid and potentially dangerous.

"Well, sure, when you say it in *that* voice."

"What tone of voice am I supposed to use when you can't even tell me the details of your contract with this guy?"

She sighs.

I sigh.

"I can't tell you the details because I signed an NDA."

"Which is weird."

"Which is not weird in this industry. I promise. Everyone who works for rich people has to sign an NDA." At least, that's what the lawyer who hired me claimed. And it makes sense. "He's just a rich, old shut in with weird dietary needs."

"That you're going to *live* with for a year!"

I roll my eyes even though she can't see me do it. "He has an estate with a guest house. It's not like I'm going to be sleeping by the fire in the kitchen like Cinderella."

"As far as you know..." Her voice trails off ominously.

"The lawyer showed me pictures of the guest house. There wasn't a stone hearth in sight. I promise."

"This guy could be anyone! He could be a serial killer."

"That's unlikely. And if he is, he's unlikely to kill me, because there's a very detailed legal trail tying me to him."

"My point is, we don't know. He could be Hannibal Lector!"

"That's a fictional character."

"He could be Sweeny Todd!"

"Also fictional."

"Okay then, Jeffrey Dahmer! He was a real person, right?"

"Unfortunately. But he was caught and died in prison. Also, why are you only naming cannibals?"

"Because those are the serial killers that are foodies!"

"I promise you, I will run at the first sign of a human femur."

There's a beat of silence and I can picture Trinity chewing on her thumbnail, the way she does when she's nervous. Then, "I'm going to miss you."

"I'm going to miss you too, Trin. But it's only for a year. And it's not like I'm moving to Antarctica. Honey Lake is twenty minutes from Austin. Forty-five if traffic is horrible."

"But you don't get a day off for a month!"

That part of the contract is a little weird.

The lawyer, a guy named Martin Harris, approached me a couple of weeks ago and offered me the job. Apparently, he knew a guy who knew a guy and law circles in Austin are pretty small. Ergo, he knew I was in deep financial waters and pretty desperate.

Is the job weird? Yes.

Were all the contracts even weirder? Yes.

I've been hired to shop for and prepare three meals a day, every day for the next year. After a month, I get two days off a month. I figure the guy I'm cooking for must be pretty old, because who else has no plans to leave his house for a solid year?

Yes, only getting two days off a month is extreme. On the flip side, I'm only making food for one guy. Only one dude.

And it's not like I didn't work seven days a week when dad was alive and I was cooking at Embarcado. Honestly, getting two days off per month is better than my usual work schedule.

Ain't gonna lie. I'm a little worried about living so far from Austin.

But also … Have I mentioned how tired I am? And how broke? And how desperate?

And how big the bonus is if I last a full year?

I'll be able to pay back my mom, with interest, and use the rest to start my own restaurant.

Okay, not like a fancy restaurant downtown. Not like Embarcado. But like a food truck or something. I haven't run the numbers yet and I'm not exactly a math person.

My half-brother, Blake, was the math guy and look where that got me.

"I'm just worried about you," Trinity says, her voice small in a way that makes me realize how long it's been since either of us has spoken. Like we've both been so lost in our own thoughts that she barely knows that she spoke out loud.

"Don't be. This is going to be great. It's exactly what I need."

And if my excitement sounds a little forced, I'm grateful she doesn't call me on it. Because I need her to be excited about it. Because I need to be excited about it.

Before she responds (excited or not), I say, "And, oh my god, if this place is anything like the pictures, you're going to die. It's gorgeous! I've got the guest cottage all to myself and there's a pool. I'll send pictures tomorrow after I get settled in."

She makes this non-answer noise that pretend conveys gushing enthusiasm. "If it's really that far out in the country, make sure not to let Mr. Sniggles outside, because I bet they have coyotes and stuff."

"I'll be careful. I promise." Like I hadn't thought of that already and lived in terror of that thought. Clearly I love my cat, but Trinity is an *animal* person. She has these ridiculous therapy chickens that she adores, so of course she'd be worried about coyotes. "Okay, I'm pulling up now," I say quickly, because I honestly can't take much more of her fearmongering. I need a pep talk here. I don't need to be giving *her* a pep talk. "I'll send pictures as soon as I have them. Love you. Okay, bye."

I reach into my bra and hang up the phone. A moment later, my phone buzzes against my tit.

Repeatedly. So I pull it out and toss it onto the empty seat beside me. From the back of the car, Mr. Sniggles makes an anxious-sounding meow.

"Please don't get carsick." I eye the pet carrier in my backseat through my rearview mirror. Because honestly, that would be the last straw.

I slow down as I turn onto the private drive leading to the Donavon estate. After several more twists and turns, the oak lined drive crests then widens to reveal a stunning view of Lake Travis. I let my car roll to a stop as I take in the view. I'm at the top of a hill, which slopes gently down to the guest cottage on my left. The main house is dead ahead. It seems to hug the cliff. Most of the house seems to be a single story, but the north wing is three floors. Its modern design gives it the appearance of badly stacked giant toy blocks. It's a house only someone very rich would build.

Not for the first time, I wonder how Mr. Donavon earned all this money.

I have no idea. Because part of my contract was a promise not to google him.

Yeeeahhh ... that was one of the weirder clauses.

But the lawyer promised me it wasn't because Mr. Donovan has a criminal background.

And lawyers never ever lie, right?

<Insert eye roll, here>

I swear to God, Mr. Sniggles can read my thoughts and is laughing his ass off in the back seat. I follow the drive until it forks, then pull up the email from the lawyer to verify which branch of the fork I'm supposed to take—it's the left one.

A moment later, I park in a spot by the most gorgeous guest house I've ever seen.

It's sleek with a mid-century modern vibe. Between the pool it overlooks, the row of sliding glass doors and the lush greenery around it, I feel like I'm stepping into a David Hockney painting.

I had planned to arrive in the early afternoon, but by the time I packed and drove out here, it's closer to dusk. It's fall, but this is Texas, so the temperature is just shy of blistering and the chirping of the cicadas is nearly as oppressive as the heat. I use the key Mr. Harris gave me to unlock the door and carry all my stuff in. I bring Mr. Sniggles in first, but don't let him out of the cat carrier until I've brought in the rest of my stuff and gotten his litter pan set up.

The house isn't big, but it has everything I need. A mud room/laundry room that leads straight off the carport. A single bedroom that's bigger than my entire shithole apartment in Austin. A bath and a half—I guess in case the guests in the guest house have guests of their own?

The full kitchen and living area face the sliding glass doors.

Even after I open Mr. Sniggles's crate, he doesn't venture out until I dump out a can of cat food onto a plate and sit cross-legged on the living room floor to lure him. He glares at me as he eats, before stomping over and curling up on my lap. I swear he only sits on my lap when he knows I'm sitting in an uncomfortable position I can't possibly maintain for long.

As I give him scritches on the top of his head, I give him the pep talk I wish my sister had given me.

"We're going to love it here. I promise. And if we don't, it's only a year, right?" When he seems to glare at me, I add in a dose of honesty. "Yeah. It's going to be weird for me, too."

two

IAN

Someone has been in my house.

I reach this conclusion based on the following evidence:

1. There is the faint, but lingering scent of lavender in my kitchen.

2. The dishwasher is running.

3. There's a smoothie sitting out on my kitchen counter.

The smoothie is still cool, but there's a definite ring of condensation on the coaster beneath it. And beneath the coaster is a note on bright pink paper.

I pick up my phone and dial my best friend. *Former* best friend.

As a rule, I prefer texting, but I find there is a degree of displeasure that can only be properly conveyed via phone call.

He answers on the fourth ring, which is unusually slow for him. Probably a sign of guilt. I don't wait for his greeting but start talking immediately.

"Why the fuck is there a smoothie in my kitchen?"

"Good morning to you, too. I hope you're doing well."

"And why is there a note attached that says, 'Let me know what else you need. Can't wait to learn your preferences'? The 'i' is dotted with a heart."

"Ian, we talked about this."

"I have no recollection of talking about this. And I have a very good memory."

"Apparently you don't. I sent you an email last week. Which was a follow up from a conversation we had a month ago. You're turning into a recluse. Which I don't really have any problem with because it means you get a shit ton of work done. Which is usually good for my investment portfolio. The last time you turned into a recluse for a year, it made it me twenty million dollars. However, as your friend, I'm worried."

"I'm fine. You know I don't like people. I'm happiest alone."

"Great. Be alone. I'm not arguing about that. But when you're alone, you eat like crap."

"I eat just fine."

"Left to your own devices, you survive solely on takeout and delivery. That wasn't a problem when you lived at the condo in downtown. Now that you're out in the boondocks full-time, it is."

"It's not a problem."

"I've seen what places deliver out there. There are exactly two places that deliver out to your house. A pizza place and some sort of weird Chinese-Mexican combo place. Even if you have them each delivered once a day, your diet would be absolute crap."

I want to continue arguing, but I can tell when I'm losing a debate and I pride myself on not falling prey to sunk cost fallacy.

Besides, he's not wrong. Anthony's New York-Style Pizza isn't half bad—given that they operate out of a gas station—until you've had it every day for three weeks in a row. As for that other place ... Chinese-Mexican fusion is a shit idea. By every standard.

"So, what's the plan here? Have you hired some full-time delivery person to bring me smoothies from my favorite shop downtown?"

I eye the smoothie skeptically. Before Martin can

answer, my stomach grumbles and I grudgingly pick it up and take a sip. It's not my standard order from Jamba Juice. It's—

The perfect combination of sweet and tart rolls over my tongue. Raspberry, strawberry, a hint of coconut. Fuck.

It's better than my standard order at Jamba Juice.

"Okay. I'll make you a deal. One smoothie, once a day. That's it."

"You tried the smoothie, didn't you?"

"Your point?"

"If you liked the smoothie, just wait and see what she can do with a proper meal."

"This wasn't delivered, was it?" I set the smoothie back down on the coaster and glare at it. I know the answer without even waiting for Martin's reply. If it had been delivered it would either be too cold or too hot by now. Plus, I recognize the glass from my kitchen cabinet. *Fuck.*

"No, it's not delivered." I can hear Martin shuffling papers in the background. "Again, we talked about this. You need a personal chef. If you're going to live like a recluse out there, you need someone to take care of you."

"That's what Maggie is for."

Maggie is the housekeeper who comes in once a

week and cleans everything from top to bottom, except my office. She worked for the previous owner and stayed on for the past two years when I bought the place.

My house is out on Lake Travis outside of Austin. I own five acres and over three hundred feet of lake-front of an inlet on the Colorado arm of the lake. There's been a house on this lot since the '50s, which is the only reason the lot is so big. The old house was demolished and replaced by a three-story limestone and glass structure that follows the curve of the cliff. The north wing of the house holds my workout room on the ground floor, my bedroom on the second, and my office on the third. The rest of the house is open concept, which means from my spot in the kitchen, I can see every square inch of my house that's not my private wing. It's the perfect house for throwing a Gatsbyesque party. Or for living like an over-paid recluse.

Wanna guess which one I am?

Even now that I live here full time, I never see Maggie. She comes on Wednesdays and the only sign I have that she's been here is the faint scent of pine when I come down from my office on Wednesday evenings.

"Maggie doesn't cook," Martin says evenly. "And you should just give up now because I already hired

Savannah. It's a done deal. She's contracted to make you three meals a day for the next year."

A suspicion creeps into the back of my mind. Besides the house, there's a pool and guest house on the property tucked away in the trees.

"Three meals a day?" I ask. "Where exactly would this person be preparing these three meals a day?"

Martin gives a beleaguered sigh. "Stop asking questions you already know the answer to, especially when you don't want to know the answer to them."

"So some woman is just living in my guest cottage now?"

"No. Not some woman. An extremely talented professional chef who is paid to live in your guest house."

"Unacceptable. Even if I was willing to have a full-time chef, she can't live here."

"Dude, you live thirty-five minutes away from the closest place of business. And that's a Valero. Having her live on site is nonnegotiable. Otherwise, she'd spend half her damn day driving back-and-forth. Besides which, those roads are winding and poorly lit. She can't make you dinner at night and then drive back to Austin. You have no clue how lucky I am to have found a chef of her caliber who's willing to cook for you out there. So don't fuck this up."

"You know how much I hate being around strangers."

"Look, I know that shit with Ava last year was a nightmare. But this woman will not talk to the press. I swear to God. She signed an NDA. I wrote her contract myself. You won't even know she's there. All you have to do is communicate with her via text and let her know your food preferences. As long as you're not hanging out in the kitchen waiting for her to show up with meals, you'll never even see her."

"I swear to God, Martin, if this shit backfires on me, I will find a lawyer better than you and sue you for everything you're worth."

"Good luck with that. There are no lawyers better than me."

"Arrogant fucker."

"Damn straight. Now, just text the woman. Let her know what you want for lunch. And you can thank me later."

Martin hangs up on me before I reply. Or tell him that if he mentions that shit with Ava again, I'll cut his balls off. Asshole.

I toss my phone on the kitchen counter and pick up the smoothie. I reread the note while I'm drinking it. What the fuck is up with the heart over the 'i'?

What is she, twelve?

I finish the smoothie, leave the cup in the sink, and head up to my home gym. After forty-five minutes on my erg machine and a shower, I'm feeling a little less grumpy.

It's not until I'm headed upstairs to my office that I realize I left my phone in the kitchen. When I grab it, I see four work messages and six from an unknown number, which I soon realize is the number from the note.

> Hi! Martin said you're usually up by seven, so I hope the smoothie was to your liking.

> I'm heading to the grocery store in a bit, so if you can send me a quick list of your dietary preferences, I can pick up food for the next couple of days.

> Also, please let me know if you will have any guests so that I can plan accordingly.

> Let me know what time you would like lunch and dinner and I will have them there in the warming drawer waiting for you.

> By the way, my name is Savannah.

. . .

Well, she's certainly a chatty thing, isn't she?

I use voice to text to send her my reply as I take the stairs to my third-floor office.

> Anything is fine.

> Except pizza or Asian-Mexican fusion.

She must've been waiting for my response because she answers right away.

I don't think Asian-Mexican fusion is a thing. But I will still try to avoid it. Any dietary issues I should know about? Anything you have trouble digesting?

> No.

Can I assume you prefer organic options when available?

> That's fine.

What about meal times?

> Noon and seven.

. . .

Since she seems inclined to repeat every question she's already asked, I get ahead of the next one.

> And I won't be having any guests for meals.

> What about caretakers? Do any of them need to eat?

> Caretakers? From the landscape service?

> Lol. No, silly. Your caretakers. Do you have staff that handles things for you?

No.

> That's awesome. Good for you.

What the fuck? Why would I need people to take care of me?

And why is she so damn chatty?

I've talked more to her today than I have to my assistant.

Of course, I haven't logged into my work computer yet, so there is that. Still, I don't want this woman thinking I have nothing to do all day but chat with her. So I send her one last text before putting my phone in focus mode.

I'll be down for lunch at 12:15. Make sure food is ready and you're gone by then.

Noted. Have a good day.

Thirty minutes later, it occurs to me she's buying groceries for me.

I open our previous conversation and ask,

Do you need money for groceries?

I find I'm oddly impatient as I wait for her answer. It doesn't arrive until 10:30.

Nope. Martin gave me cash for this week and is arranging a credit card for me for expenses.

I don't think of the woman again until I break for lunch at 12:45 and find a Panini in my warming drawer. There's bacon, cheese, and some kind of creamed spinach concoction on sourdough bread. It's maybe the best thing I've ever eaten.

I hate dealing with other peoples' stupid mistakes.

The only thing I hate more than that is dealing with the consequences of my own stupid mistakes.

And when it comes to this personal chef, I was wrong, and Martin was clearly right. The asshole.

texts between ian and savannah

I haven't heard from you in a couple of days. How has the food been?

Fine

Any special requests in the coming week? I'm going to the store this afternoon.

No

You've had smoothies for breakfast every day so far. Would you like to try something different?

No

What about flavor profiles? Any of the smoothies strike your fancy?

They are all fine.

IAN HAS SILENCED NOTIFICATIONS.

Great. 😐 I'll assume everything I'm making is perfect. 😄😅😂🎉

I'll just keep pulling recipes out of thin air.

Dinner will be at 7 PM as per usual.

texts between ian and savannah

SECOND WEEK

Since I've had no complaints, I'm going to assume that the meals have been fine.

Please let me know otherwise.

If you have any preferences, any meals that you have particularly liked, I would love to hear them.

It would help me meal-plan for the week.

Everything is fine.

IAN HAS SILENCED NOTIFICATIONS.

texts between ian and savannah

THIRD WEEK

Same as usual, right?

Are you doing this on purpose????

Food is fine. Everything is fine.

All work and no play makes
Savannah a dull girl.

I don't mean to sound bitchy and complain about what is a pretty sweet gig here, but Mr. Donovan is weird.

Also, I'm assuming I can say that to you and that it's not a violation of my NDA, because you're his lawyer and you know he's weird.

Please be advised: I am his lawyer. I'm not your lawyer. You can't just say anything, even to me.

So did I violate my NDA just now?

I'll give you a pass on this one. Technically, you're not supposed to talk about him with anyone.

Okay. Fine. I see your point. But I have to talk about him with someone.

No. No, you really don't.

Yes, I do. What if I'm worried about him? You know I'm not a trained medical professional, right?

Obviously.

I'm hired to cook meals for him, nothing else. Right?

Yes. As per your contract.

It's just that sometimes I text him and he doesn't text back for a really long time and it makes me nervous.

So I have no way of knowing if he's… I don't know, fallen in the shower or something. Died in his sleep. Been abducted by aliens.

I have no way of knowing.

Why would he-died-in-his-sleep be your automatic assumption if he doesn't text you back?

I don't know. Doesn't that happen sometimes to people who are …

you know. His age.

You bring food to him every day, correct?

Yes. As per my contract. Three times a day.

And when you return for the dishes, has he eaten the food you left?

Yes. Obviously. If he hadn't, we'd be having an entirely different discussion.

Then it's fine.

It's not fine! What if he dies and no one but me is there and I don't find his corpse for a week?

What then?

Because if I'm responsible for finding his rotting body, I will not be okay.

Do you hear me?

Have you ever watched one of those forensic shows on tv? Do you know what happens to a dead body if it's left undisturbed?

At some point, it explodes.

Or maybe that's only if it gets too hot.

My point is, I will not be OK if I have to find his body exploded all over the interior of the house.

I

Will

Not

Be

Okay

Are you even listening to me anymore?

Yes. I'm still here. I was just checking on something.

I discussed it with Ian.

He will text you back at least every third day. And if there are two or more meals that he has not eaten when you return for the dishes, you have permission to call 911.

You do not have to go search for his body yourself.

Great. That is such a relief. Knowing that he could die in that house, and I won't have to be the one to find the body. Thank you.

You're welcome.

I was being sarcastic.

Yes. I got that.

Do you have any other requests?

You know, while he is freshly traumatized by the image of you discovering his bloated corpse. Might be the right time to ask.

As a matter of fact, yes. If you could get me a list of his preferences, that would be great. Right now, I'm flying blind. I have zero clue what he likes or doesn't, and it's making me insane.

He hasn't given you any feedback about what he likes?

No. The times I've texted him about it. All he says is it's fine.

I'll handle it

texts between martin and ian

And you've complimented none of her cooking?

I pay her so that I don't have to compliment her.

Like I said, absolute ass

Like I said, obviously.

What's your point?

Clearly you think her food is amazing. So you should at least tell her that.

I didn't say her food was amazing.

Exactly. That's my point. You haven't said it. Not to her. Not to me. But I know you love her cooking.

You wanna know how I know? Because the second day she was cooking for you, I asked how it was and you told me to fuck off.

Your point?

I am your closest friend. Maybe your only friend. And the only time you tell me to fuck off is when you're pissed off because I'm right and you're wrong.

That's not true.

Why are you having such a hard time admitting that hiring her was a good idea?

Fuck off.

Just grow a pair and tell her which of the meals you've liked. Because right now you're making her job harder.

If I do that, will you finally fuck off?

Yes

Fine

texts between ian and savannah

texts between ian and savannah

I heard a crashing noise from outside. Are you okay?

Are you okay?

Do I need to call 911?

I'm fine.

Sorry for the delay in replying. My cat nearly escaped when I was carrying out your lunch.

I dropped the dishes and they broke.

I'm so sorry. Lunch will be delayed about an hour while I make you a fresh plate. You can deduct the cost of the broken dishes from my paycheck.

Don't worry about the dishes. Whenever is fine. Just shoot me a text when the food is ready.

Is your cat okay?

Yes. Thank you for asking. He gets bored and tries to take advantage of me whenever my hands are full.

I didn't realize you had a cat

I was allowed to bring him according to my contract.

No. It's fine. I just didn't realize. Does he try to escape often? Because there are coyotes out here. And bigger things. It's not safe.

Yes. I know. This is the closest he's come to making it out. I will be more careful in the future.

Wait. What bigger things? Like wolves?

Possibly. But more likely bob cats and cougars.

There are wolves, bob cats, and cougars out here???

I didn't realize you were carrying my food back and forth each meal.

Yes. I am.

It would be more logical for you to cook in my kitchen from here on out.

My contract says I should be in your house as little as possible.

I'm not inviting you to hang out, merely stating that it would be more convenient for both of us if you were to use the kitchen in the main house, which is undoubtedly better equipped.

You still aren't cooking in the kitchen downstairs.

It can't be convenient to carry a fully prepared meal from one house to the other three times a day.

It will be less convenient to haul the raw ingredients back and forth.

Martin will arrange to have the kitchen in the main house fully stocked by lunchtime tomorrow.

I don't mind cooking in the smaller kitchen in the guest house and the walk isn't bad.

I do mind that my food isn't as fresh as it could be.

Furthermore, I am unaccustomed to having my direct orders disobeyed.

I expect all meals to be prepared in the kitchen of the main house from this point on.

IAN HAS SILENCED NOTIFICATIONS.

three

SAVANNAH

"Unaccustomed?" I mutter under my breath as I drag myself down the path from my cottage to the main house at six o'clock the following morning. "Who the fuck uses the word 'unaccustomed' in a text message? Rich wanker."

It's not that I haven't been getting up at six every morning for the past six weeks to make his smoothies. I have.

Five forty-five almost—*almost*—feels like a humane time to drag my ass out of bed at this point.

But it's different when I get to stay in my cottage. I get up early. I stumble around for a half hour, bleary-eyed, while I make coffee and stare into the abyss of the freezer while waiting for inspiration to hit. Most mornings, by the time I'm hitting pulse on the blender, I'm practically alert.

A quick hike down the path to Mr. Donovan's house to drop off the smoothie in the fridge and I'm legit ready to start my day.

But this?

This feels different.

Probably because he's ordering me to do it.

Definitely.

The past six weeks have been ... weird.

For the first time in my adult life, I've been getting enough sleep.

I've been exercising. I've been reading for hours every day. Thanks to the cottage's huge TV and indulgent streaming subscriptions, I've watched more TV than at any other time in my life. I've caught up on the entire Marvel Cinematic Universe and practically every notable TV show of the past decade. Game of Thrones. Black Mirror. Curb Your Enthusiasm. The Witcher. Law and Order.

Do you have any idea how much TV you have to watch to catch up on Law and Order?

A lot.

You have to watch a troubling amount of TV to catch up on Law and Order.

Honestly, I have too much free time on my hands.

Of course, for the first time in my adult life, I'm not hemorrhaging money. I'm making over ten thousand dollars a month and have virtually no living expenses. I've already paid my mother with interest.

Now, if I can just keep myself from climbing the walls. Somehow I always thought that if I ever got cabin fever, it would involve fewer actual cabins.

I guess there is one good thing about Mr. Donovan telling me to cook in his kitchen. I'm facing the challenge of creating a brand new cooking space.

As for Mr. Donovan himself, I don't quite know what to think of him. Taciturn and grumpy, for sure. I still haven't so much as laid eyes on him. Sometimes I hear footsteps from the floor above. And maybe a rowing machine?

I suppose he must be fairly fit for such an old codger. Not only does he live in a house all by himself out in the middle of nowhere, but it's a house with three floors.

With all of my recent spare time, I've been reading more and listening to podcasts. One of them was about the health benefits of using stairs daily. So maybe he's like one of those hundred-year-old women who lives on the isle of Santorini and walks up and down the mountainside every day to stay healthy.

Of course, chances are I'll never see him. I'll know nothing about him other than that he likes tacos and panini's.

I let myself into the house at exactly six thirty and make my way straight to the kitchen. Until now, the most I've done is leave food in the warming drawer.

It doesn't take me long, however, to find the blender and dump in the ingredients for a smoothie. Strawberries, a banana, coconut cream, local honey, collagen powder (because I assume at his age, he needs all the joint health he can get), powdered vitamin D (because I have yet to see him leave the house, so he must need that as well.)

The wing of the house is all one open space. The front door sits in the dead center of the back wall, with the kitchen to the left, a sprawling living room to the right, and an endless wall of floor to ceiling windows looking out on a sliver of yard before the cliff drops sharply off to the lake a hundred feet below.

On the far side of the kitchen, there's a hall that leads to the private wing of the house. I assume. I've never ventured beyond the warming drawer. The view of the lake is absolutely stunning. The sun is just creeping over the hill as I hit pulse on the blender.

The grinding breaks the silence. Predictively, food catches in the mechanism. I release the pulse button, add another dash of coconut cream, and grab a wooden spoon to shake things up a bit. Just as I go to pulse again, a hand grabs my shoulder, turning me around. I glimpse a tall, broad-chested man. Someone young and fit. Clearly, we're being robbed.

I act instinctively, whacking him over the head repeatedly with the wooden spoon. He grabs my hand to stop me. I grab his arm and turn around, putting my back to his, crouching low to flip him over my head the way I learned in self-defense class.

It doesn't go quite as planned. I don't know if he took the same self-defense class I took, or if he's just that much bigger than I am. I stomp on his toes, trying to jab the wooden spoon into his eye from behind me. All the while yelling, "What did you do to Mr. Donovan? Who are you? Why are you here?"

There's a series of huffs and grunts from behind me before I find myself wrapped in his arms, completely at his mercy. Oh my God! What if this is the guy who taught my self-defense class? What if he teaches those classes just to mess with women so he can rob them later?

"Stop trying to—"

I stomp on his foot again.

"—kill me."

"Never!" I scream defiantly, stomping all the harder.

Which would be significantly more effective if I wasn't barefoot.

I squirm in his grasp, trying to kick at his legs. "What did you do to Mr. Donovan?"

"I *am* Mr. Donovan."

It takes a few more seconds of futile squirming for his words to sink in. Gradually, I still.

He's got his arms wrapped entirely around me, one around my waist, just beneath my breasts that's latched onto my right wrist. The other around my chest and holding onto my left arm to keep me from gouging his eyes out. My feet are entirely off the ground and dangling uselessly.

After a moment of breathing heavily in my ear, he asks, "If I let you go, are you going to try to kill me again?"

"Yes."

He gives an indignant huff.

"I mean. No. If you can prove you are who you say you are and you haven't murdered poor Mr. Donovan."

"I am Mr. Donovan," he repeats, lowering me so

that my feet touch the ground and then slowly releasing me.

I whirl to face him, wooden spoon still raised, to see him backing away from me, hands raised at his side like he's surrendering. I get my first good look at the guy.

He's about my age, maybe just a smidge older than my twenty-seven, but it's hard to say. He's taller than my own five-eight by at least five inches. He's broad chested and dressed in a grey Henley and —dear God, help me—gray sweatpants. He's got near black hair that's standing up on end. He's just shy of traditionally handsome. His eyebrows are too bushy, his nose is too big, with an odd bump that makes me think he broke it at some point. But his eyes are soulful and his lips impossibly sensual. He smells like sleep with just a hint of cedar. He's barefoot and rumpled, like he just rolled out of bed, but he has pink smoothie all over him because I attacked him with the spoon.

"I was just about to escape," I say.

His hands drop a little and his lips curve into a smirk. "Obviously."

I narrow my gaze suspiciously. "Prove you are who you say you are."

He drags his thumb across his cheek to scrape off

a dollop of smoothie and then sucks it off. "This is my house. Why should I prove who I am?"

I broaden my stance and pull back the spoon a notch. "This is Mr. Donovan's house. He's an elderly recluse. And you're ..." I give him a once over. I'm aiming for scornful, but it probably comes off as lecherous. "And you're not."

He stills, returning my gaze, but keeping his PG rated. "What?"

"Mr. Donovan," I insist slowly. "Is an elderly recluse."

I am not entirely sure why I'm arguing with this man so insistently.

Even as the words are leaving my mouth, I know I'm being ridiculous.

But I just ...

I can't reconcile this man standing before me with the man I've been imagining for the past six weeks.

This man is ... okay, I have to admit it, to myself if not out loud... ridiculously hot. He is not elderly. He is not feeble. He is not an old codger.

"Mr. Donovan is an elderly recluse," I say one more time, and if I had ruby red shoes I could click while I say it, I would do so.

The man in front of me rolls his jaw in obvious irritation. "I am not elderly."

"Are you Mr. Donovan, though?"

"Obviously."

"Then prove it."

"This is my house. I woke up to find you making a smoothie in my kitchen. Which I assume means you're Savannah. If you'll just put down your weapon—" he says weapon with a heavy dose of disdain. "—I'll get my wallet and show you my driver's license."

four

IAN

It shouldn't matter to me how beautiful she is—Savannah, this woman who is my personal chef and living on my property. It shouldn't matter at all, but somehow, now that I've seen her, it does.

For the life of me, I don't know why it does.

I almost never even notice what other people look like.

After nearly six months of dating Ava, I couldn't even remember what color her eyes were. I objectively knew she was beautiful because other people kept telling me she was. Now, after two months of not having seen her at all, I have only a vague recollection of blond hair. And a lot of high heels. I only remember her name being Ava and not Eva because that's how my assistant saved her contact on my phone.

So trust me when I tell you, I don't normally study women, let alone notice their beauty.

Despite that, I can't stop looking at this woman.

Maybe it's because she's here in my kitchen, dressed in a tank top and impossibly short shorts. Barefoot, for fuck's sake.

Maybe it's because I only just woke up and my brain is still foggy with theta brain waves and the wash of hormones that accompany morning wood.

Maybe it's because I haven't even actually met her, but I've already held her in my arms, tight against my body, her ass rubbing against said morning wood.

Or maybe it's just her.

Just some primal, gut level reaction to this particular woman.

Whatever the reason, I seem to take in everything about her all at once, and she is stunning.

Long legs that are tan and lean and shapely, despite the lack of heels. Hips and tits that are full of soft, enticing curves. Skin that smells faintly of lavender. Hair that is brown and half piled on her head in some kind of sloppy knot. Eyes that are the most stunning blue-green I've ever seen.

I swear I've never once even noticed another person's eyes before. I've never just stared into them, lost in the pale green flecks scattered amongst the blue. The dark ring around the outside of her iris. The way her eyes dilate as she studies me in return.

Everything about this woman tugs at something deep inside me I would have sworn didn't even exist until this moment. Something that makes me want things I've never wanted before. Not like this, at least.

I'm a grown man. Obviously I've felt physical attraction before. The simple, base reaction to another human's body. But not like this. This is something different. This sudden need to ... what?

Pull her back into my arms? Feel her ass bucking against my dick again? Get another lungful of her hair?

"Show me," she blurts.

Her words jolt me back into the moment.

Show her?

Show her all the things I want to do to her?

No.

That can't be right.

"If you're really Mr. Donovan, then show me your ID."

A beat passes as her words sink in.

Right.

She doesn't believe I'm ... me. And I offered to get my wallet and show her my ID. But all I want to do is stand here and stare at her like a fucking moron.

Jesus H. Christ. What is wrong with me?

"Right. My driver's license." I scrub a hand down my face. Get more smoothie on my hand. A streak of it right across my palm. She's still standing between me and the sink. I stare at my palm for a second, at the ice-cold line of pink smoothie, and I have the absurd urge to excuse myself to the bathroom so I can jerk off.

Seriously.

What the fuck is wrong with me right now?

Desperate to get the smoothie off my palm before I do something really stupid, I just lick it off.

Which is a mistake for two reasons. One, this smoothie is my new favorite flavor and I instantly want to pour it across her bare thighs and lick it off her skin. Two, she's watching me as I do it.

I don't know this because I'm watching her as I do it. For some inexplicable reason, I can't seem to look at her now that I've catalogued her every feature. But I know she's watching me because I hear her gasp.

Which I'm guessing she does because she's

horrified or offended. And she still thinks I'm a murderer.

"Right. I will be back." I turn, stalk a couple of steps back toward my suite. Then stop and look back at her. She's still standing there, wooden spoon held up, defensively, looking like she's ready to bolt. "Wait right here."

In my bathroom, I wash my hands, give my dick a squeeze, just to curb the ache, and splash some cold water on my face.

My cock is still hard as a fucking lead pipe—which I hope to God she didn't notice earlier—so I splash more cold water on my face. I try to distract myself by thinking through the proof of Fermat's Last Theorem. And then Polignac's conjecture.

I have got to get this under control, because I'm her employer, for fuck's sake.

And I know I'm not the kind of man any normal woman would want to be with. Hell, everyone who has an internet connection knows that. Despite my net worth. At least, that's according to Ava. Who is the only woman I've dated long enough to have an opinion.

Luckily, just thinking about Ava and her widely voiced opinions is enough to kill the remains of my chubby. I grab my wallet off the table by my bed and head back to the kitchen.

I find Savannah pacing the length of the island like it's a racetrack, wooden spoon still in her hand. She must have set it down at some point and then picked it back up, because the smoothie she was making is now in a glass, the counter has been wiped clean, and the blender is rinsed and sitting in the sink.

Which is more an indication of how long it took me to get my body under control than of her efficiency.

I yank my driver's license out of my wallet and toss it on the counter beside the smoothie without looking too closely at her.

"I'm sorry I startled you."

Even though I'm trying not to study her, I can feel her gaze on me as she inches closer. She doesn't pick up my driver's license, but pulls it across the counter until it's close enough to look at before nudging it back in my direction.

She lets out a huff of air that morphs into a chuckle. "No. I'm sorry." She points at my head with the spoon, then realizes she is holding it like a weapon and throws it in the sink. Crossing her arms over her chest, she props her hips against the sink and faces me. "I don't know why I kept insisting you weren't Ian Donavon. You were just not what I expected."

She kept insisting I was old. Which makes zero sense.

I'm still standing by the doorway, trying to give her plenty of space, even though I'm fighting the urge to pace. To fidget. To do anything other than stand here with my arms awkwardly hanging by my sides.

"Why did you think I was elderly?"

"I don't—" She gives another chuckle. This one sounding more nervous than confused. "I don't know, actually. It must have been something Mr. Harris said that made me think it."

"You didn't recognize me?"

"Should I have?" She sounds baffled. "I mean, there was a clause in my contract that said I wasn't supposed to google you. Or read up on you. So I didn't."

"Right." Martin said he'd included that in the contract. I just assumed it was a bullshit clause included to make me feel better. It never occurred to me he'd actually found someone to work for me who hadn't heard of me before.

Which, in retrospect, is obvious arrogance, assuming that everyone would know who I am. Or maybe just a sign of how insulated the tech industry is. It's been years since I've met anyone who didn't know me by reputation. Who didn't already have opinions about me, my reputation, or my business.

And that was before Ava and I started dating, which threw me into a whole new social circle. Suddenly, I wasn't just one more guy making too much money in a tech field. I was a guy dating a gorgeous, up-and-coming actress.

Never mind that she wasn't up-and-coming until we started dating. Suddenly I was interesting to people outside my industry.

Then we broke up, and she used her "broken heart" to launch her career.

Sure, there are hundreds of mediocre actresses starring in low-budget indie movies every year. Only those with stories of wild breakups with tech billionaires get invited to speak on late night talk shows.

Not that I'm actually a billionaire. That's just a phrase gossip pages like to throw around, because "tech billionaire" is pithier than "dude who got lucky and made a couple hundred million dollars."

Martin and my mother both tried to tell me it wasn't as bad as it sounded. Maybe they were right, because now, here is this gorgeous woman, standing in my kitchen, and she's never heard of me.

Not that it matters one way or the other.

Because she's still my employee.

And even if *she* hasn't heard the things Ava said about me to anyone who would listen, *I* have.

Selfish. Arrogant. Socially and romantically obtuse. Cue the coy smile at the camera. *If you know what I mean.* Cue laughter from the talk show host. Cue another smile, this one a little sad. *But also just lonely. So I tried. I really did. But in the end ...*

Those are the things she said in public. She wasn't so coy or polite in private.

So, no, it doesn't matter how beautiful Savannah is.

Or how unsettling it is to see her bare feet on my kitchen floor.

She is an employee. And she doesn't deserve a boss who gets a chubby every time he thinks about the raspberry smoothies she's been making him.

Which I now undoubtedly will for the rest of my life.

Fuck my life.

"You said I should prepare your meals here."

This time, when she speaks, I look at her, only then realizing how long it's been since I said anything.

Because of course it has been. Because I'm doing this all wrong. This being a normal human thing. This thing I always seem to fuck up.

"Yes," I say, because she paused like she was

waiting for me to speak, but I'm not sure what else to say.

"Should I do that? Or have you changed your mind?"

"Yes." Something I can't read flickers across her face and I realize I answered the wrong question. "I mean no. I haven't changed my mind. You should cook here. It's only logical."

I think back to the text conversation we had just yesterday. Before I knew the gentle slope of her shoulders in a tank top and the lavender scent of her hair. Back before I worried about her cat sneaking out and being eaten by a coyote. Back when it seemed foolish for her to prepare my meals in another building and then bring them here to reheat. Of course, that still seems foolish.

Having her cook here is still the logical decision. So logical, in fact, that I can't believe I didn't say something earlier.

Maybe that's part of the problem. Maybe if I had met her when she first came to work for me, I wouldn't feel awkward now.

Yes. That must be it.

It's less that she's so stunningly beautiful and more that it took me by surprise.

Now that I know what she looks like and now

that I expect her to be in my kitchen, it won't be a problem. Familiarity and contempt and all that.

I give a terse nod and turn to leave, only stopping when she asks, "Don't you want it?"

Her words send off a flood of images through my mind. All the things I want from her. All the ways I want her.

Which is ridiculous since I've spent less than ten minutes in her company so far.

I turn back around to see that she's closed the distance between us. And is holding out the smoothie she made for me.

I clear my throat. "Yes. Of course."

I take the smoothie and book it out of the kitchen as quickly as possible.

I make it to my office on the third floor before it occurs to me to wonder what the hell I'm going to do with this smoothie that I certainly won't be able to drink.

five

SAVANNAH

After the great smoothie debacle, I panic.

Meeting my employer should not freak me out, but it does.

I run back to the cottage, hastily pack my belongings, and spend thirty minutes trying to coax Mr. Sniggles out from under the bed.

The problem is, Mr. Sniggles hates car rides. And he hates when I pack. The fact that he equates the two things and has realized that one will lead to the other is a sign of his pure feline genius. It is also the only thing that saves me from utter humiliation. By the time 8 AM rolls around, my back is twinging from lying on my belly. I have not yet coaxed Mr.

Sniggles out from under the bed. I have, however, inhaled a great number of dust bunnies.

Eventually, I'm forced to acknowledge the truth. Unless I want to call my sister and have her drive all the way out here to help me corral Mr. Sniggles, I am not leaving today.

I get up, pull out a notebook that I use to write down recipe ideas, and start making a pros and cons list. Blank page, line down the middle, pros on one side, cons on the other. And it's a no fail approach to decision making.

Con: my employer could be a serial killer, and since I can't google him, I have no way of knowing.

Though, now that I think about it, googling him wouldn't actually give me that information, anyway. If he's a known serial killer, he would already be in jail. And if he's not, then that's probably not information provided in his LinkedIn profile.

Pro: I'm making the best money of my life.

Con: possibly because my employer is a serial killer

Pro: I have a lot of free time. More than I've ever had in my adult life.

Con: there is at least the possibility that so much free time is driving me insane. Which is why I suspect my employer is a serial killer

Pro: if he is a serial killer, wouldn't he have

already killed me? If he was going to. Assuming he's a serial killer who hunts close to home. Which I'm pretty sure none of them do.

Pro: my boss is hot. Total eye-candy, for sure. And he smells delicious.

Con: he's my boss, therefore it doesn't matter if he's hot.

Con: aren't serial killers always hot? Or was that only Ted Bundy?

After a few minutes of staring at the list, I'm disturbed by two things. One, I am clearly watching too much TV. Particularly too much Law and Order, because my imagination has taken a decidedly dark turn.

Chefs—even head chefs who work in a restaurant owned by their father—don't make great money. As a result, I've spent most of my adult life living in a series of shit-hole apartments in not-great parts of town. Which means statistically speaking, I was more likely to be killed by a serial killer at any other time in my life than today.

Again, I blame Law and Order.

You know what's even worse? I didn't worry about any of this until this morning when I met him.

Am I truly worried that he's a serial killer or am I merely disconcerted by how easily overpowered I was? Or am I disconcerted by how... disconcerting I found him?

I hate to admit it, but I'm afraid it's the latter.

And I have to admit, I liked the idea of him being an old man. I liked the interactions we had when I pictured him as grumpy and feeble, tottering around that big empty house alone. I felt like I was doing something good in the world. Like I was helping someone who needed me.

Maybe I have daddy issues?

I nearly laugh out loud.

Obviously, I have daddy issues.

If I didn't have daddy issues before, I certainly do now. I spent my entire childhood and teenage years trying to earn my father's approval, and I thought I had. I followed in his footsteps. I worked at his restaurant, earning less pay than anyone who knew I was his daughter thought I should. I assumed that if he were to die suddenly that I would inherit at least half the restaurant.

It wasn't anything any of us had ever discussed. But that was just what seemed fair.

When he dropped dead of a heart attack at 65, I found out that the restaurant was in Blake's name. My father hadn't even made a provision for me to stay on as head chef.

Yeah. I developed some daddy issues real

fucking fast. Some my-half-brother-is-an-asshole issues, as well.

My pros and cons list isn't getting me anywhere. I pour myself a cup of coffee and I'm staring out the window of my little cottage when I see a car zip past.

The cleaning service comes every Wednesday like clockwork. And they drive a red truck. This was a white car; Tesla, if I'm not mistaken. Which means Ian Donovan has left his house for the first time since I've moved in.

Where is he going? Is it a coincidence that he's leaving on the same day we met? Or are the two things related? Did he spend his morning making some insane pro/con list also?

I'm sure he didn't. Why would he?

If he did, what does that mean?

six

IAN

Just because I don't like to leave the house, doesn't mean I don't like to drive. Quite the opposite, in fact. The rare occasion when I leave, I absolutely love to lose myself behind the wheel of a car. I just don't do it very often.

After meeting Savannah for the first time, I try to resume my morning routine. I row on my erg machine for ten minutes instead of my normal twenty. I take a cold shower, but can't seem to get the water cold enough. It seems like nothing I do can scrub away the image of Savannah in my kitchen.

I go to my office and log into my computer. I sit

staring at the screen for what feels like hours. I roll out my yoga mat and meditate for what feels like hours. Eventually, I get up and I pace. More hours pass. Except when I look at my watch, it's been less than thirty minutes since I got out the shower.

Fuck.

That's when I decide to go for a drive.

I don't bother changing clothes before heading out to the detached garage that's not quite visible from the house. I grab the key fob for the Tesla model X off the wall and head out. I immediately use the voice to text to send a message to Martin.

> Clear your calendar for lunch. I'm heading into town.

I glance down at the navigation center and see that I will arrive at Martin's office in less than an hour. I sent another text.

> Make that coffee. I'll be there before ten.

A few minutes later, my phone lets me know that I have a text from Martin. I never changed my settings, so my phone reads the text aloud in the default, feminine Siri voice.

> What the hell, dude?

> A little heads up would be nice. I do have other clients, you know.

I send a message back.

> None of them pay you as much as I do.

> All of them pay me as much as you do.

> OK, none of them have made you as much money as I have. Do you have an hour for me or not?

> Fine. I'll shuffle things around.

I've almost reached Highway 71 when another message comes through. I'm so used to the back-and-forth with Martin in my car, That I'm surprised that this message isn't from him.

It's from Savannah.

For a second, I'm tempted to pull over and read the message on my phone myself instead of having my phone read it for me. I resist the temptation.

> I just noticed your car leave the driveway. Will you be back in time for lunch?
>
> I'm only asking so I know whether or not to prepare food for you.
>
> Not for any other reason.
>
> Obviously, your time is your own.

By the time several moments pass without another text from her, I'm wishing I had pulled over to read them. I can't get any sense of her tone from the Siri voice and somehow it's jarring hearing a message from her read with the same flat delivery that Martin's messages are read in.

Which is stupid, because it's not like I know Savannah. I've only met her once. And they're fucking text messages. It's not like I could hear her tone by reading them, anyway.

Or that I would have the emotional sensitivity to interpret her tone of voice, even if she was standing right in front of me.

That I'm even thinking about shit like this is a sign of just how off kilter I am.

I dictate a message back before I can let this woman get even more in my head.

I'll be out for lunch, but back by dinner.

Should I say something more?

Should I apologize for not telling her I would be out for lunch?

Fuck.

Pissed off that I'm even thinking about this, I tell my phone to silence notifications and crank up some Nirvana. My car is equipped to self-drive, but that feature keeps the car driving the speed limit, so I don't turn it on. Besides, the point of driving—instead of calling a driver—is to feel the car and the road and the acceleration. By the time I'm on highway 71 heading towards Austin, I almost feel like my normal self.

Martin's office is in a skyscraper downtown. It's in one of a pair of buildings called the Prescott towers. One tower is offices. The other is a hotel.

Thank God, they offer valet parking, because traffic in downtown Austin is always a goddamn nightmare and parking is even worse. When I make it up to Martin's office on the top floor, his assistant shows me in right away.

Surprisingly, the rest of the law firm's office is empty. When the assistant leaves, I throw myself into the chair and start talking before he even looks up from his computer.

"Where the hell is everyone else? Does no one else in your office even show up anymore?"

His hands still on the keyboard, then he pushes back in his chair before turning to look at me, slowly arching one eyebrow.

"It's Sunday."

I blink. "Really?"

Martin smirks. "Yes. Really."

"If it's Sunday, why are *you* in the office?"

"Because my asshole best friend who I haven't seen in two months messaged me first thing in the morning and said he wanted to meet me. That's why."

"Then why was your assistant here?"

He quirks an eyebrow. "Because I pay her very well to come in on Sundays if I need her to. Since you have literally never demanded to see me on such short notice before, I didn't know what the hell was up."

"You could've said it was Sunday and told me to fuck off." And then I think about the message he sent me saying he had to move some things around. "Do you normally work on Sundays?"

"No." Then he shrugs. "Okay, sometimes."

"Were you working today?"

"No. I was not in the office before nine this morning."

"Then what things did you have to move around?"

"Well, there were three women in my bed when I woke up, so I had to move them around to get up."

"Seriously?" Although I've been best friends with Martin for nearly a decade, neither of us engage in locker room talk. If he's regularly with three women at a time, I've never heard about it before now.

"No. Not seriously. Jesus, don't be such a dumb ass." He scrubs a hand down his face.

"So it was a business meeting you had to move?"

"No. It was one woman." He holds up a hand as if staving off my next question. "And before you go to the trouble of pretending you're interested in my love life, it was one and done, and I'm probably never going to see her again."

"I'm doing it again, aren't I?"

"What?"

"That thing that I do. Where I'm an annoying asshole without realizing it."

He makes a show of glancing at his watch. "Well, you've only been here for 10 minutes so far and you already realized it, so maybe we're making progress."

"You know," I grumble. "You're not such a joy to be around yourself."

"Nonsense. I'm a ray of fucking sunshine."

I just raise an eyebrow at this because I'm not sure whether he's joking. And if he's not, would it be polite for me to correct him?

I mean, I suspect he *is* joking, but I don't know for sure.

"You going to tell me why you're here?" he asks.

I prop my leg up on my opposite knee, feeling it bounce as I clench and unclench the arms on the chair. It's a wooden chair. The kind they used to have in libraries all over the country. It's no frills, just sturdy oak. I like that it feels solid beneath me. That it's no-nonsense. Like Martin.

Although I like his office, I like Martin, and being here is no more unpleasant than being anywhere else, I'm still not exactly comfortable.

"If you don't wanna talk about it–"

"I met Savannah."

"Oh. I see." He leaves it at that.

I suspect the fact that he doesn't follow up with any of his usual bullshit is a sign that he hears all kinds of implications in my tone that I wish he didn't.

But, I guess if I didn't want him to know that meeting her in person was a big deal, I probably shouldn't have insisted on driving into Austin on a Sunday and dragging his ass out of bed.

He says nothing, but waits patiently for me to continue.

Eventually, I do. "You should've told me how beautiful she is."

"Honestly?" He leans forward, propping his elbows on his desk, and gives me a look I can't quite read. Which is not fucking surprising, since I can never read anyone's expression. "I didn't know you would notice she's beautiful."

"She's fucking gorgeous. Those eyes of hers…"

There's an end to that sentence that I don't finish. Something about how I could get lost in them. About how I want to stare into them for hours. Something poetic and well thought out that I don't have the words for.

"Have you met her?" I ask, suddenly picturing Savannah as Martin's hook up. I hate the thought almost as much as I hate the knot of something unpleasant that forms in my stomach as I imagine the two of them together.

"Yeah, I met her," he says simply.

"How?"

"I heard about her situation from …" He trails off for a second, frowning like he's searching for the right word. Which is odd, because Martin always has the right word. He clears his throat. "I heard about her from an acquaintance."

"What's her situation?"

"You know I can't talk about my clients."

"Is she your client?"

He shrugs, admitting that she's not. "She was involved in a nasty lawsuit. It should've been an open and shut probate case. Her representation fucked things up. By the time she figured it out and fired the guy, she had a shit ton of legal bills. I figured hiring her as your personal chef would kill several birds with one stone."

"That's uncharacteristically altruistic of you."

"What can I say? No one can be an asshole 100% of the time."

I think about the things Ava said about me. "I think some people would argue with you on that point."

Martin's gaze darkens, like he can see where my thoughts are heading.

Before he can say anything else, I ask, "Can you tell me anything more about the case?"

"Not much. If you're curious, ask her yourself."

I snort. "Yeah. Because that's something I'm going to do."

"It could be. You're a curious guy and you don't like unanswered questions."

"Right. Because I have such a long history of starting conversations with beautiful women."

"Do you realize that's the second time you've called her beautiful?"

"Is it?"

Honestly, I'm kind of surprised I've only said it twice. Martin and I sit in silence for several long moments. It's one thing that I like about Martin—his ability to tolerate my weird silences.

We met back in undergrad at the University of Texas. We lived on the same floor of one of the smaller dorms. He was pre-law. I was in computer science. Somehow, we both ended up in a dorm with mostly liberal arts and theater kids. I've always suspected he befriended me solely because I was the only person who wasn't always inviting him to improv classes.

Lost in my own thoughts is pretty much my default state. What's unsettling is that this morning my thoughts are still about Savannah.

What was the lawsuit about? How did she end up a personal chef? What was she doing before this?

Before I saw her standing in my kitchen this morning, I honestly had given little thought to her at all. Food appeared. I ate it.

Was it better than what I had been eating? Yes.

Unquestionably. Every bite she prepared was delicious. I just never thought about it.

I don't like that having seen her in person makes me think about it. I don't like that her appearance affects how I feel about her food or about anything else.

I don't know how much time has passed when Martin speaks again. "You know, it is okay to find a woman beautiful. It's okay to notice that about her."

Maybe for guys like Martin. Guys who have more experience with beautiful women. Guys who hook up with women on Tinder. Even back in college, Martin had the kind of easy charm that won people over. Sure, he's gotten a lot grumpier over the years. He's got family shit going on that I wouldn't wish on anyone.

But when he wants to, he can win over anyone. He is the opposite of me in that way. There's nothing easy about me. Nothing charming. Nothing personable.

I make a noncommittal sound. After a few minutes, I struggle to put what I'm processing into words. "It bothers me."

"What does?"

"I didn't think about her at all until I knew what she looked like. I didn't even wonder what she looked like until I saw her in my kitchen this morning."

"Why does that bother you?"

"Because I thought I was a better person than that." Martin just quirks an eyebrow, his lips twitching like he's trying not to laugh at me. "Okay, I know I'm an ass. I just thought I was an ass who wasn't shallow. I never notice what people look like. I value ideas. Intelligence. Contributions to society."

Of course, Martin knows all this about me. He's been my best friend since college, so these questions of ethics and values are familiar territory. It's the kind of thing you hash out over beers late at night when you room with someone for years.

Still, I feel like I have to defend my line of thinking, even though he doesn't ask it of me. "I guess I've been okay being a known ass, because at least I wasn't shallow. After Ava broke up with me and started talking shit in those interviews, I could justify it. Fine. I'm a jerk. I am arrogant and impossible to get along with. It didn't matter what she said or thought because I had the moral high ground."

"You know Ava is a selfish, petty bitch, right?" Martin's voice is uncharacteristically harsh as he says this.

"Yes. That's what you keep telling me."

"I can't be the only one who tells you that."

I resist rolling my eyes at his tone because I know when I'm being coddled.

"My mother has brought it up as well."

He snorts. "That's ironic. Wasn't she the one who introduced you?"

"Yes." And encouraged me to date her as well. There was a long lecture about grandchildren. "But apparently she changed her mind about her after the interview in Vanity Fair."

"There you have it. The two people you trust most in the world agree she's a bitch."

While I trust their opinions, I also recognize that they both emotionally invested in me.

So, of course, they think Ava is a bitch. That doesn't mean they're right.

Martin leans back in his chair again, giving me a thoughtful look before he asks, "So if this isn't about Ava, what is it about?"

"I don't know." And I guess that's what bothers me. I'm not used to not knowing how I feel about something.

Truth is, I'm not used to having feelings about things.

It's unsettling.

It's distracting.

It's unacceptable.

"I'm going to fire her," I say, suddenly decided.

"Savannah?"

I nod, the uneasy tension in my stomach unraveling now that I've decided. "Yes. I'll just let her go."

"You can't."

"What?"

"You can't fire her." Martin grins. "Technically, you're not her boss. I am."

"That can't be right."

"Unfortunately for you, it is. A year ago, you decided you didn't want to be burdened with inconsequential activities, like paying your property taxes and your electric bills. You asked me to draw up paperwork putting me in charge of managing your properties. Which I did. It's part of why you keep me on retainer. It's how I hired Savannah for you. Ergo, you are not her boss. I am. Ergo, you can't fire her."

"Fine. Then *you* fire her."

"I'm not going to. Regardless of how you feel about her personally, she's done nothing to justify letting her go. She's an excellent chef. She's doing her job. The job that she needs. And I'm not gonna fire someone without cause just because you think she's pretty." He leans forward, working an eyebrow. "And if you can't see why it's wrong that you're even asking me to, then I might need to suggest some sexual-harassment training for you. As your friend.

Not as your lawyer." Then he shrugs and adds. "Both, actually."

I frown and cross my arms over my chest. Because I know he's right and that I'm being a total dick. Still, I push back half-heartedly. "If you wanted to, you could come up with some reason to fire her."

"Yeah, maybe. But I *don't* want to." There's a gleam of determination in Martin's eyes that even I can see.

Annoyed, I stand. "Fine. I'll just have to figure out how to tolerate it."

I'm almost out the door when he says, "You know Ava was full of shit, right?"

I turn back to look at him. "We covered this already. She was a petty bitch, etc. etc."

"Yes, but she was also lying. She was never with you out of pity. She was with you because she wanted to be. It just pissed her off you didn't care."

I consider his words for a moment, rolling them over in my brain to see if they make sense. "So you're saying the problem wasn't with her, it was with me? The problem was that I was a bad boyfriend?"

He shrugs. "You probably were a bad boyfriend. I won't argue with you about that. It's not in your nature. Ava knew that going in. She just thought she could change you. She thought she could make you care about her. When she couldn't, it pissed her off. That's on her, not you."

"I guess it's a good thing you're my lawyer and not my therapist, because as far as pep talks go, this one is total shit."

"You're not paying me to give you pep talks. But if you were, consider this: just because you never cared enough about Ava to put in the effort, that doesn't mean you won't ever care about anyone else. You're a smart guy. Beyond smart. If you wanted to be a good boyfriend, you could learn how."

I think about Martin's words all the way back home. Maybe he's right. There are a lot of things that I didn't know how to do. Programming came naturally to me. It always has.

Business? Finance? Not so much. But I had an idea for an app that would help people manage their money. I had the knowledge and skill to build it. I could have sold it and moved on to the next big idea, but I didn't want to do that.

I wanted to run my own company. I wanted to build something from the ground up that I was proud of. I wasn't going to hand my baby over to someone else until I could get what it was worth.

So I learned the rest. I either taught myself or hired people to teach me how to get venture capital, how to become a CEO, how to run things myself.

If Martin is right, I could learn how to be a boyfriend as well. If I wanted to.

Which sounds like a great idea in theory.

But here's the bit Martin is forgetting.

I worked my ass off on Cookie Jar for a solid decade. And then one day, I realized it bored me. I'd done all the things I wanted to, I had a buyer offering me a shit ton of money, and I was just tired of playing CEO.

So, could I learn to be a great boyfriend? Yeah. Do I want to? Nope.

Ava and all her drama cured me of that.

It's a moot point anyway, because no one—not Ava, not Savannah, not anyone else—is even asking that of me.

Besides, I like my quiet life out by the lake just as it is.

I like the solitude. I just need to ignore the fact that there's a beautiful woman living on my property and cooking me meals.

If I have the option of putting forth the effort to learn how to be a good boyfriend, or to learn how to forget she exists, I'm gonna choose the latter. Not because it's easier on me, but because it's easier on her.

seven

SAVANNAH

Hours later I'm still ... flustered.

And I'm fully ready to admit that I am being ridiculous.

Okay, so my boss is hot. Big deal.

Just because I pictured him as old and weird, like some sort of modern, American Miss Havisham—and then he turned out to be no such thing—that doesn't mean I should quit. After all, many people have hot bosses. It happens to the best of us. Just because *I've* never had a hot boss before, means nothing. Especially given that all of my previous bosses have been family members.

Obviously, the thing I most want to do is Google Ian Donovan.

I can't do that, because if I do it will void my NDA and my contract. Voiding my contract and saying goodbye to the rather sizable bonus I'll get at the end of the year. There's no point in even staying if I don't get the bonus. Which means I can't Google him.

So what am I supposed to do? Just... exist, not knowing who he is?

When I thought he was old and ill, his behavior made sense. Maybe not great sense, but at least I could understand it. Now that I know he's young, fit, and hot, nothing about this situation makes sense in the least.

He seemed surprised that I didn't recognize him. Which means he's either delusional or famous. Which does me absolutely no good in narrowing down who he actually is because I have spent the past two decades of my life in a weird foodie bubble. The only famous people I know are celebrity chefs.

He is definitely not that, because if he was, he wouldn't have needed to hire me and he wouldn't say things like "tacos are fine."

Everyone knows tacos aren't *fine*. Tacos are the best.

Finally, I break down and call Trinity, who asks

how my life in isolation is going and then, before I can answer, launches into a tirade about Blake, which ends with, "Blake clearly wasn't hugged enough as a child." Trinity's tone is harsh, and I appreciate the defense, even though it treads closely on an issue I've been considering lately.

"Honestly, I don't think any of us were hugged enough as a child." That's one of the problems with having so much damn time on my hands.

Problem? Blessing?

One or the other, I still haven't figured out which.

Basically, I've spent way more time lately thinking about ... well, stuff. All the little traumas and emotional wounds that no one makes it out of childhood without incurring. And all those moments in our childhood that created this wedge between Blake and Trinity and I. The wedge that led us to this moment.

"True," Trinity agrees. "Dad certainly wasn't affectionate with any of us. But only one of us turned out to be an absolute total wanker."

"Yeah, about that–" I begin before her use of the word wanker hits me. Then I practically squee. "Oh my God, you've been reading it?"

A beleaguered sigh comes through the phone.

"Yes, I've been reading that fanfic you recommended." She sounds absolutely horrified to admit it.

"And it's amazing, right? So good!" Yes, that's the other thing all this free time has led to.

I started with rewatching all the Harry Potter movies on HBO, which led to the books. And eventually to Dramione fanfic.

"I swore I was done with that world," Trinity grumbles.

"I know, I know. You don't support J. K. Rowling's opinions. It's not about that. Particularly not when you delve into the fanfic."

"Yes. I know. And I agree. There are so many people writing in that universe, it's not about just Rowling anymore. But I can't believe you, of all people, got me into reading Dramione fanfic. You were never even a Harry Potter fan. You were always too busy hanging out at the restaurant with dad to even read the books. When you were ten, I asked you what you thought your Patronus would be, and you asked me if a Patronus was one of the five French mother sauces."

"What can I say? I was an ignorant twat as a child. I'm clearly much more sophisticated now."

"You don't get to take that superior tone of voice when you've been reading Dramione smut."

"It's not smut. It's amazing. And you've clearly

also been reading," I point out as I flop back onto my bed inside dramatically. "And isn't it the best?"

"Yes. I have to admit, it's amazing. Loads better than when I went through that horrible Twilight fanfic stage."

We talk for a few more minutes about fanfic before Trinity brings the conversation back around to the real reason for our call. Even though I didn't say it out loud, she's my sister, and sometimes there are just things sisters know.

"How is the job going?"

"It's going well. Really well."

"But..." She leaves the question dangling there in the air between us for a minute before I answer.

"But things aren't exactly as I thought they were."

There's a bit of silence that feels fraught with Trinity's desire to say, I told you so. Instead, she says, "If you're in danger, no amount of money is worth—"

"It's not like that." At least, I'm ninety-nine percent sure it's not like that. Ian doesn't seem dangerous—moody, an absolute wanker, and not at all what I expected—but certainly not dangerous.

After all, if he was dangerous, wouldn't I already be... I don't know? Dead, or something?

I was completely at his mercy. Despite my delusions of self-defense, he incapacitated me almost immediately, and could've done much worse than he did. If he was prone to fits of rage, or had any interest in violating me somehow, surely, he would've done it when I was beating him with a wooden spoon.

"No, it's nothing like that. But the other day I actually met my boss, and he wasn't exactly what I expected."

"Wait. What? Do you mean you hadn't met him until now?"

"I hadn't. The specifics of my contract said that I should stay out of his house as much as possible. So I made food in the cottage, brought it over, and left. I was never in the house over five minutes at a time. The other morning I met him and he's not what I expected."

"What did you expect? How is he not what you expected?"

"I don't know why, but I assumed he was old."

"He isn't?" There's a bit of silence, and then she adds with a chuckle, "I guess I thought that, too. You kept describing him as a shut-in."

"Exactly. Who our age lives in total isolation? In a house like this?"

"A house like what?"

I can hear the curiosity in her voice, but I'm

already shaking my head, even though she can't see me. "You know I can't give you details. But he can afford a personal chef. And I've sent you pictures of the cottage, so you can let your imagination fill in what the main house looks like. And whatever you're picturing, it's that and more."

"And he's our age?"

"Approximately. I don't know for sure."

"So ..." She lets her voice trail off.

"So, what?"

"What's he look like? Is he hot?"

Gah. How am I supposed to answer that? What can I say here?

If I say he's average, she'll know I'm lying, because Trinity has younger-sister-Spidey-sense. If I say he's hot, I'll never hear the end of it.

And is he actually hot? I don't know. He's tall and fit. And he smelled amazing. Since I have to say something, I say, "I don't know. 'Hot' is such a weirdly subjective word."

"So, in other words, yes, he's hot. Where does his money come from? Is it like inherited old money? Is he European royalty? Is he in the mafia? A hired killer?"

"That's just it. I don't know. And you know *I* can't Google him to learn more about him."

"Yes. I know. That was the thing I think is so

weird about your contract. You should be able to Google anyone you want. Even your boss."

"Well, when I thought my boss was a codgerly, old shut in, it didn't matter that I couldn't Google him. I assumed I wouldn't find anything."

"Obviously, you were going to find things. Otherwise, why would there be a clause that you couldn't Google him?"

Huh. That was a good point. Damn Trinity and her logic.

"Anyway, my point is I can't Google him. And I can't tell you who he is."

"Well, you're not giving me a lot to work with here." Her tone is exasperated.

"I know. I just... Never mind. I guess I just needed to say it out loud. How much I wish I could tell you who he is and have you Google him for me. Not because I need to know details, but just so that I know that there's nothing that I would wish I had known later. If that makes sense."

"Yes. It does." There was a long moment of silence in which I can practically feel Trinity's frustration pulsing through the line. Finally, she says, "I talked to Mom the other day."

"How is she?" I ask even though I talk to mom regularly.

She always tells me she's doing great. But I can

hear the strain in her voice. I know how much it hurts her, this mess that Blake got us all into.

It's ridiculous, but I think she blames herself somehow, for not realizing what an asshole he'd become, even though none of us saw it either. Even though she's not his birth mother, she raised him from the time he was ten. She loved him like he was one of her own until dad died and Blake took over the restaurant and screwed us out of our part of dad's inheritance.

It seems to hang between us every time I talk to her. The way Blake betrayed me. The way I asked for money from her and she gave it to me. It all just feels like this thing that is between us that neither of us can get past.

"She's doing well," Trinity says. "She told me you paid her back."

I squeeze my eyes closed and try to keep my voice as neutral as possible when I say, "I guess I should've told you she loaned me money."

"No. You didn't want me to know. It's fine. I can't say that I blame you. I think if things were reversed, I wouldn't want to admit it either."

Which I guess is as close as Trinity is ever going to get to telling me she thinks I'm an idiot.

"I just... If there is anything I can do, you'll let me do it, right?"

"Absolutely."

"If you've already paid back, mom, there's no reason you have to finish this contract."

Instead of replying, I change the subject. "Remember when we were kids and you and I used to pass messages back-and-forth?"

She chuckles. "The coded messages?"

"Yeah. Those. We thought we were so clever."

"Yeah, what about it?"

I look down at the piece of paper in my hand where I have been scribbling a message in several versions, trying to make the words sound right. I haven't found a combination yet that doesn't sound ridiculous.

Sighing, I fold the page in half and close my eyes again. "No reason. I was just thinking about it the other day and wanted to make sure you remembered."

We talk about other things for a few minutes. It's not until we're off the phone and I'm starting prep for dinner that I let myself think about her question. I paid back Mom. I am—almost—out of debt at this point.

I still have the lawyer's bills. I'll probably have those for a long time. But paying mom back was the important part. At least to me. As for all those legal fees, well, I could always declare bankruptcy. Not my favorite choice, obviously, but not the end of the world either. I wouldn't be the first or last chef to do so.

If I really felt like I was in danger—if I was really worried about my safety—obviously, I would turn and run. I wouldn't feel like I had to stay just for the money. That's not what bothers me. What bothers me about the situation is the fact that I feel like I want to stay. Now that I know Ian Donovan isn't some elderly recluse, now that I know he's young, fit, and strangely, compellingly attractive, I don't feel like I have to stay, but I want to. He's a mystery I want to unravel. A question I want the answer to.

That's the real problem. Not that I feel like I have to stay, but that I want to. I want more information. Why does he live in this huge house all by himself? Why doesn't he go into town more often? Why didn't he want me to Google him? Why didn't he want me to know who he really is?

These are the questions whirling in my mind as I make his evening meal and walk it down the hill to the big house. Even though I saw his car return during the afternoon, I don't see him in the house.

After I've eaten my sandwich by myself in front of the TV, I take out the piece of paper again and stare at it. Letting the words roll over in my mind. I type out a text to Trinity, and then I delete it. I go to bed, leaving the sheet of paper on the counter in the cottage.

That night, I have the strangest dream. I dream that I'm a house-elf at Malfoy manor, but I am also Hermione Granger. And when I'm ordered to bring food for Draco, it isn't Draco at all. But Ian Donavon. What an absolute wanker.

eight

SAVANNAH

The Monday after Smoothie Sunday, things return to normal. Sort of. If anything about this situation can be considered normal.

On Sunday, I prepared his meal in my cottage like I've been doing.

I didn't intentionally ignore his request to cook in his kitchen. At least, I don't think so.

But when wake up in the morning, I find a text from him.

> Is there a reason you didn't make dinner here?

I stare at the message for several long moments while I scramble for an answer.

Yes. Obviously, there's a reason.

I didn't want to run into you again.

And I don't want to spend my days wondering what it is you do and who you are. My life was easier when I thought you were just an elderly shut in and I didn't have to wonder about you.

In the end, I keep my answer simple.

No. Just habit.

Good.

I'll expect you to cook here starting tomorrow morning. You can have groceries delivered to this location if that helps.

I'll have eggs for breakfast from now on.

Eggs?

Six weeks of smoothies every morning and now he wants eggs? That can't be a coincidence.

How would you like them prepared?

It doesn't matter.

So, as per his instructions, I cook in his house. I don't see him, but I grumble under my breath the whole time.

Who doesn't have a preference on how they eat their eggs?

Who?

I've been making eggs since I was nine and everyone I have ever known is picky about their eggs.

There are infinite varieties: poached, scrambled, soft-boiled, hard-boiled, fried, omelets.

So there's no way he doesn't have an opinion on how he likes his eggs. So why not just say how he likes them?

Is he fucking with me?

Beyond the egg-related text, I don't hear from Ian again for several days. I'm nervous every time I let myself into his house and jumpy the entire time I'm there. Despite that, I'm too much of a smart ass to just let the egg thing go. I serve him a different egg dish for breakfast every day, each more elaborate than the next.

A classic Denver omelet, followed by migas, a quiche, and then chilaquiles. I end the week with a soufflé. Why, yes, I do have to get up at five thirty to have his soufflé on the table by seven. Totally worth it.

I still have so many questions about him and no way to get answers—not without violating my contract and risking losing my bonus.

Who is he really?

Where did all of his money come from?

Why does he live all alone in the middle of nowhere?

And who has no preference in how they eat their eggs?

Maybe he's a cyborg?

A terminator sent from the future?

An alien sent here to study human dining habits and learn how humans like their eggs?

At least I've moved away from all the serial killer themed options.

I still haven't googled him. If I'm going to live and work in the middle of nowhere for a year, there's no way I'm going to do anything that might void my contract.

I haven't given up on the idea of sending a coded message to my sister asking her to Google him for me. I just haven't figured out the phrasing of it yet. Every time I come up with something that I think might work, I scribble it down on a piece of paper I keep folded in my pocket. I have a running list on my phone. The problem is none of my options sound like real sentences.

In Another Neverland. Don't Occasionally Notice ...?

See? That's not a sentence.

Iced Avocados Notably. Devour ... ?

That one's even worse.

I'm making dinner on Saturday night—Bolognese on capitelli, with a blue cheese-arugula salad, and a bottle of Cabernet) when I get a text from him.

I have my earbuds in and I'm listening to Taylor Swift, so I get a ding from my phone when the text arrives.

> I'm coming down.

> Try not to attack me.

Huh. That almost sounds like a joke.

Do cyborgs have a sense of humor?

I suppose it depends on their programming.

The sauce is simmering away on the stove and I've been chiffonading the basil. I turn off Taylor and pull out the earbuds just in time to look up and watch him enter the kitchen.

"It's a good thing I warned you I was coming." His gaze drops to the chef's knife in my hands. "That knife would've done more damage than the spoon."

I set the knife down and step away from the cutting board, my lips twitching at his joke.

Despite his dry tone, that was a joke, right?

In the week since I've seen him last, I convinced myself that my imagination had run away with me. That he couldn't possibly be as attractive as I remembered.

Which is funny, because I've never really thought of myself as having an active imagination. Not like Trinity. Until now, I've always been the practical one. Now I'm the one with fantasies full of serial killers and cyborgs. And men with unruly hair and mesmerizing blue eyes.

Ian isn't classically handsome. There's nothing clean-cut about him. No lantern jaw or chiseled cheekbones. Instead, there's rumpled softness to him. His hair looks like he's been running his fingers through it all day. His jaw, like he hasn't shaven in days and did a poor job of it even then. He seems like a man who gives no thought to his looks whatsoever.

But I'm not fooled by his sloppy appearance.

When you work in the food industry long enough, you learn how different bodies carry weight. A tailored jacket or a well-cut T-shirt can hide a multitude of sins.

Ian doesn't use any of those tricks. From the way his shirt hangs from his shoulders and his pants sit low on his hips, I can make some guesses about Ian's physique.

Whatever he does when he's not eating my food, he burns a lot of calories doing it. He has the countenance of an absentminded professor and the body of a triathlete.

However, the illusion of the rumpled, eccentric slacker is ruined when I meet his eyes.

When we met a week ago, he seemed confused, a little befuddled. Today, his gaze is intense and unyielding.

"Did you need something?" I ask, wondering if my egg-based teasing went too far. Maybe I shouldn't have poked the bear.

When he didn't comment on the first couple of egg dishes, I just kept pushing.

Except instead of bringing up the meals I've been serving, he holds something out to me.

"I found this in the trash last night."

I barely glance at the slip of paper in his hand. "You go through the trash?"

"No. It was on top."

Only then do I glance down at what he's holding. It takes me a second to recognize it as a page torn from my notebook.

He extends his hand, and I take the paper from him, reading the words aloud. "Fish tacos with chipotle slaw and pickled onions. Fried green tomato and bacon panini with roasted potatoes.

Pasta Primavera with summer squash." I look it up at him, frowning. "Is there a problem with next week's menu?"

"On the other side."

I flip over the note and my heart stutters.

Innocuous Answers Never. Don't Over Notice Animals Veering Ominously Nowhere.

Innocent Alligators Notch. Dalmatians Only Newly Anticipate Vocal Overtones Nightly.

I consider feigning innocence, but I doubt he'd fall for it. So I simply arch an eyebrow and say, "Yes?"

"It's obviously a code."

In for a penny, in for a pound. I nod.

"Of my name."

"It is."

"Why?"

His gaze is moving over me, seeming to take in every detail of my appearance. It's unsettling. But that's not surprising, since everything about this man unsettles me, and in none of the ways he should.

Including the fact that I'm not even tempted to lie to him.

"I assume you've seen my contract?"

He gives a tight nod.

"Then you know I was told not to google you."

"Yes."

"And I haven't. Not before I signed the contract and not since. But..."

"But?"

"I didn't mind. When I assumed you were just some old, rich guy living alone, it didn't seem important. I thought you were eccentric, yes, but that wasn't even the weirdest part of the contract."

"And now?"

"Since we met, I have questions." Since he just keeps staring at me, I start babbling. Trying to unravel the thoughts in my head that haven't even made sense to me yet. "My sister and I used to do this thing when we were kids and we spent summers apart. She always stayed with our mom. I would go visit our dad. She and I would send messages back-and-forth." I laugh nervously. "I don't know why we thought it was important to keep them coded or why we thought they wouldn't be able to break our code. It was very Parent Trap of us, I suppose."

He looks down at the paper again. And then back up into my eyes. "The first letter of each word to spell out a word. Punctuation indicates a new word. Easily deciphered. It's a childish code."

I chuckle, and this time it's with genuine amusement, because *that's* what worries him about this?

My lack of cryptography skills? "Well, we were children."

"So you sent your sister my name in code so that she could dig up information on me and report back to you?"

"No. Not yet. I couldn't figure out a way to make your name into a sentence that wasn't obviously gibberish."

"Isn't the obvious gibberish the point? How would she know it was a message if it was a sentence that made sense?"

His tone is harsh, like he's more upset about my lack of originality than he is with my snooping. I'd like to see him do better with his crappy name.

I bump up my chin and meet his gaze defiantly. "I never sent the message. I haven't violated my contract. You have no reason to fire me and no reason to withhold the bonus."

"I'm not going to fire you." Something about the way his eyes flash when he says it makes me think he's surprised that he admitted that out loud.

"Then what? Why bring it up to me?"

"Why didn't you just Google me?"

"Because I need this job. I need the money from the bonus. And I wasn't sure..." I shrug, giving a vague gesture to the house. "I don't know what kind of surveillance techniques rich people have to watch their employees. I thought there would be some fancy tech way you were tracking what I was doing. It didn't occur to me you would just look in the trash."

"If you wanted to know who I was, why not just ask? And why wait until now?"

"I thought if you go to the trouble of hiding your identity, then you must really not want me to know who you are. Your identity didn't seem to matter when I thought you were old and fragile. Now it does."

He's frowning, clearly confused. I don't want to come out and say it. *Now that I know you're young and hot, it's much harder not to stalk you online!*

Pretty sure admitting that would be the fastest way to get me fired from this cushy job that I desperately need to keep. Thankfully, I've been mentally rehearsing my excuse.

"Now that I've seen you in person, now that I know you're—" I gesture to his shoulders and his height. "big and strong, it seemed unwise to just live here on your property without knowing more about you."

"Unwise?"

"I'm a woman living alone on the property of a man she knows nothing about. Miles from civilization." He's still frowning. Still clueless. So I spell it out for him. "In the case it wasn't obvious to you, you overpowered me."

"You're afraid of me?"

He sounds appalled.

"Not exactly, but you're obviously stronger than I am. And I don't think of myself as a weak person. I don't think of myself as small and fragile. But you…"

You make me feel small and fragile. Delicate. Defenseless. But not in a bad way.

Which is the most alarming part of this entire situation.

I should be scared of him and I'm not. He could overpower me, but I trust him not to. I have this baseless, instinctual trust in him.

"You're afraid of me." He repeats again. Suddenly those eyes that looked so hard and unyielding just a moment ago flicker with something I can't read.

I feel like I kicked a puppy.

Before I can deny it, he pulls out his own phone, types on it, and then hands it to me. I take it from him automatically, glancing down only briefly before looking back at him.

He must see the question in my eyes, because he says, "There. You haven't googled me. I googled me."

"Okay. I'm confused. What do you want me to do?"

"Read. Whatever you want. For as long as you want." He gestures to a stool on the other side of the island like he wants me to sit. Once I'm sitting, he eyes the food on the stove suspiciously. "Will that...?"

He doesn't seem to have the vocabulary to form the question he's trying to ask.

"It's a Bolognese sauce. It needs to simmer for another 30 minutes, anyway. I'll stir it every few minutes."

"No. You read. I'll stir."

He turns his back to me like he's giving me privacy with his phone. He picks up the spoon and starts stirring with a sort of methodical intensity. You'd think he was in potions class.

God, I really need to find things to read that aren't fanfic.

Luckily, my boss has given me plenty of material. I look down at his phone. The number of search results is staggering. The top one is a Wikipedia article so I start there.

IAN DONOVAN IS AN AMERICAN entrepreneur best known for creating the financial services app COOKIE JAR.

My gaze jerks up to take in the man standing with his back to me.

Cookie Jar?

I have that app on my phone. Everyone I know has that app on their phone.

Well, probably not *everyone* I know. Everyone of my generation, at least.

It's a combination banking, investing, and financial literacy app. I've used it for nearly a decade.

I reread the first line of the article that mentions his birthday. He's a couple of years older than me, but he still must've started the company when he was barely out of college. Or even before.

I skim the rest of the article, but see nothing that hints at why he's so secretive. Or why he's living out here all by himself. Why he never leaves the house.

I click back to the page of results. There's a profile on the Washington Post. Several things from Forbes magazine. An article in the Wall Street Journal about the sale of the company. A couple of articles about women he's dated. Beautiful, semi-famous women.

Not an out of work chef among them. No surprise there.

None of the articles are from the past couple of months.

Occasionally, I glance up to see him still standing there, stirring. He says nothing, but I can see the tension in his shoulders. The stiffness in his posture.

Something about the way he's standing now reminds me of how I used to feel when I cooked for my father. The way my stomach would clinch nervously as I waited for him to taste the food I prepared. Waited for him to judge my talent. My skills. Me.

Waited to hear whether he would deem me worthy of his approval and affection.

I clear my throat. "Thank you. For trusting me with this."

He carefully sets the wooden spoon down and then turns back to look at me. His expression is cautious and shuttered. Like he's waiting to hear my verdict.

He's clearly expecting...

What? What does he think I read in here that would make me judge him?

I know more about him than I did before, but somehow I got the answers to none of my questions.

I still don't know why he's isolating himself. Why he lives alone. Why he didn't want me to know who he is.

"Is it because of the money?"

"What?"

I put the phone down on the island between us and nudge it back in his direction.

"You're clearly rich." According to the article in

Forbes, very rich. Insanely rich. "Is that why you didn't want me to know who you were? Because you're wealthy and you're afraid people will ask something of you?"

He makes a noise that's something between a huff of indignation and a scoff of disdain.

"Did you watch the interview with Ava Grayson?"

"No." I merely glanced through the article that mentioned they dated. And I didn't watch any videos at all. Other than the quiet bubbling of the sauce and the occasional thud of the spoon against the side of the pan, the kitchen has been completely silent.

"You should watch it."

"If you can hand me my earbuds..." I nod toward my phone and earbuds that are sitting beside the stove.

"Just play it." His tone is harsh again. Bitter. "Start just after the three-minute mark."

Immediately, I click on the video. I automatically turn the volume down and it still feels unnaturally loud in the silence of the kitchen. I move the video along, stopping at just before the three-minute mark.

"We'll get back to your new movie in a minute,"

the interviewer is saying. "But first I want to ask you about your love life."

Ava Grayson gives a diffident laugh, like the question surprises her. "Yes. My love life has been ... quite dramatic lately."

"I understand you just broke up with tech magnate Ian Donovan."

"Yes." She nods, looking forlorn.

"And what was that like? Rumor has it he's a genius."

"Undoubtedly." Again with a sad smile. "It's difficult to talk about."

A box of Kleenex appears as if out of nowhere as the camera zooms in on Ava.

She pulls one tissue from the box with a flourish and dabs at her eyes. "Yes, he's brilliant. But cold. Hard to live with. Difficult. After a while, I just couldn't ..." She trails off dramatically. I push pause on the video. She said nothing but implied a lot. I put the phone back on the counter and look up to see him watching me.

I piece together the timeline I'm making in my mind. Brilliant young guy builds an app and then a company that makes him hundreds of millions and puts him on the map. He sells the company. Dates a beautiful up-and-coming actress for a while. They break up. He becomes a recluse.

Or maybe he sold the company after they broke up. I would need to check the dates on that and I don't want to go to the trouble while he's watching me.

Either way, his current self-imposed solitary confinement definitely started post break-up.

That's what this was about?

A bad break up?

Oh, People Magazine ... you lying bastards. Rich people are not like us after all.

My worst break up happened two months after my dad died.

Dan and I had been dating for about a year. We worked together and lived together. At some point, I sold my car to save money. Because our shifts at the restaurant were similar enough, it made little sense for us to keep two cars.

He broke up with me three weeks into the probate case, as soon as he realized it wasn't going to be a slam dunk. He saw the writing on the wall before I did. Or maybe he was just less invested.

My point is this: when Dan and I broke up, I lost my home and my transportation. Just after having lost my father and my future.

I had to hire an Uber to move out. Anything that didn't fit into that Uber stayed with Dan.

The day I moved out, I cried in the shower at my

new place, then I got dressed and made it to work on time. Where I had to work with Dan.

Maybe it's a sign that I was more emotionally invested in the restaurant than I was in my relationship with Dan, or maybe I really am the heartless bitch he accused me of being.

Maybe I shouldn't be so quick to judge.

I slide Ian's phone across the counter back towards him. "Thank you for…" I'm not sure how to end that sentence—or what exactly I am thanking him for—so I just leave it dangling.

One thing is for sure: he really loved her.

I don't know why that makes me sad, but it does.

I need you to amend Savannah's contract to take out the clause that says she can't google me.

It's Savannah now, is it?

What? No response? You can't take a little teasing?

I didn't realize that required a response.

You're no fun.

That's not news to anyone.

OK, you want me to amend the contract. Am I allowed to ask why?

She's afraid of me.

What?

It makes sense. She's a single woman, living in an isolated area, on my property. The situation was making her uncomfortable. So I gave her permission to do whatever research she wanted.

Got it.

Also, take out the NDA. She should be able to talk to whoever she wants.

What? What the hell is going on over there?

Did you sleep with her?

No.

Jesus. Why would you even ask that?

Because you just told me to burn her NDA.

Your point?

You've always been fierce about employees signing NDAs.

Even before this shit with Ava.

Given this sudden, drastic change in attitude, I think it's a reasonable question.

Fuck off.

If you've slept with her, I need to know. As your lawyer, I need to be able to protect you. If you'd brought me into the loop with Ava, before things got serious, I could have helped.

Fuck.

Off.

I'm serious.

So am I.

Okay then, as your friend.

I'm worried. This isn't like you. Even with Ava, you had an NDA.

You're the one who hired her. You're the one who refused to fire her when I came to you last week.

Is that supposed to make me less worried that my best friend and most important client is acting out of character?

Fine.

No, I didn't sleep with her.

Okay. Then why not just tell me that?

Because it's a stupid fucking question.

I just don't want her to be afraid of me.

Despite what Ava thinks, I'm not an insensitive monster.

I thought we agreed Ava was the monster.

Also, I'm not burning the NDA. But I think she has a sister she's close to. I will amend the NDA to give her permission to discuss you and her employment with her sister, contingent on the sister also signing an NDA.

Um ... why have I been contacted by some asshole lawyer telling me to sign an NDA?

Wait. What?

Who?

Martin clucking Harris

He says he represents your employer

Um. Yeah, that's the lawyer who hired me.

Let me get this straight

Martin clucking Harris is the lawyer who hired you to work for your mysterious boss?

Yes. Why?

And why do you keep calling him Martin clucking Harris?

No reason

It's a small clucking world, is all

Wait. Do you know Martin Harris?

How?

No. Maybe

Cluck

I thought I knew him, but maybe I don't

It doesn't matter

Just tell me about this NDA

Huh ... let me check.

Okay. Yeah. I guess my employer 🙄 thinks I should be able to talk to you about him.

Can we all just agree rich people are weird?

And that's not a violation of my NDA because all rich people are weird. Not just the one I work for.

Okay, I signed the NDA. Now, can you tell me what this is all about?

My employer is Ian Donavon. And he's not elderly or feeble like I thought.

Wait

Your boss is Ian Donovan?

Yes.

The Ian Donovan? The guy who founded the Cookie Jar?

Yes.

And is worth like a gajillion dollars?

I don't know his net worth and I don't think I could discuss it if I did.

<GIF of Chris Evans laughing>

What? Why is that so funny?

<GIF of Jennifer Lawerence spewing tea>

Is this helpful?

Because I feel like this is not helpful.

OK...

But, just hear me out

You thought your boss was some creepy old recluse, but he actually looks like this

<GIF of Ian Donovan in a suit>

I hate you.

No, you don't

In fact, I'm your favorite sibling

You are my only sibling who hasn't taken me to court

That's fair

Still, I can't believe you knew your boss was Ian Donovan and you didn't realize he was the owner of Cookie Jar.

I knew you'd been living under a rock for the past two years. I just didn't realize the rock was that big and heavy

Shut up.

So… How hot is he in person?

Because he looks really hot

I don't know that I'm comfortable discussing the hotness of my rich boss with you.

Noted. So? Very hot

I didn't say that.

You didn't have to. You implied it

I don't see how I implied he was very hot because I didn't wanna talk about it.

I'm your best friend and your sister, and I know everything you're thinking. All the time

Pretty sure you don't know what I'm thinking right now.

Yes, I do

You're thinking I'm a pain in your ass and you're sorry that you have to talk to me about him

And you're wishing that annoying lawyer hadn't asked me to sign an NDA because then you would have a reason not to.

And you might be imagining stabbing me

Not to death, but with something pokey and painful like chop sticks

Okay, so you do know what I'm thinking

So, what are you gonna do?

About what?

About the fact that you have a crush on your hot boss? Your hot, rich boss

I don't have a crush on him.

<GIF of Carol Kane screaming "liar"
>

Whatever. 😒

Are you going to tell me what the deal is between you and Martin Harris?

What? No smart ass quip?

My point is, he's my boss and I need this job. So there's nothing to do

Um.. yes there is. You get after it

I'm not going to get after it. 😒

Why not?

He's hot. You're into him

And you're never into anyone

That's not true

I just got out of a long term relationship

A) that was more than a year ago

B) that wasn't a relationship

I'm pretty sure it was

No. That wasn't a relationship. That was a long term living situation that was convenient because Dan never pushed you for more than you wanted to give

Okay… that's hurtful

I'm not judging you. I'm just saying, you deserve better. You deserve sex with your hot rich boss

Well, it's not happening because my boss may be hot and rich but he just got out of a long term thing and I think she really broke his heart

So? Be his rebound girl!

I deserve better than to be a rebound girl

Agreed

But you also deserve hot sex with your hot boss

> I'm officially ignoring you because you're being ridiculous.

SAVANNAH HAS SILENCED
NOTIFICATIONS.

nine

IAN

I was ten when I realized I make people feel uncomfortable.

Or rather, I was ten when I realized exactly how uncomfortable I make most people feel.

I had known for years that I wasn't exactly normal. When you start kindergarten understanding long division, it's not exactly something you can hide.

But my mother always told me I shouldn't try to hide it. That I was exactly as smart as I was supposed to be, and it wasn't my job to make other people feel comfortable with that. What can I say?

My mom made it seem like being on the spectrum was cool long before it became a thing on TikTok.

It wasn't until after my parents split up and my dad started dating that I knew any differently. It was one of his girlfriends who made me realize it.

"He's just creepy," I overheard her tell my father once. "The way he just stares at you without blinking. It's unnatural."

She was the first of his many girlfriends. After I overheard their conversation, I told my mom I didn't want to visit my dad again, but she said I needed to try. So, it seemed worth my time to figure out how to not be creepy. How to make people feel comfortable enough to stick around. It turned out to be a moot point because he didn't want to spend time with me anymore than I wanted to spend time with him and his rotating vapid girlfriends.

My point is this: you can learn how to do almost anything with enough determination and unlimited time on the Internet.

By the time I started Cookie Jar, I thought I was doing an admirable job of pretending to be a normal human. It was exhausting, but I could do it.

Except all that shit happened with Ava.

Why the hell was I working so hard to be normal, if it would never be enough?

So I made a deal with myself. I was done pretending to be something I wasn't.

My mom had been right all along. It's not my job to make other people comfortable.

It's not my god damn job.

It's not.

So why the hell am I tip-toeing around my own house? Why am I hiding in my office every time she comes to the house?

Whatever the reason, more than a week has passed since the night I realized Savannah was afraid of me and I gave her permission to google me.

If she didn't know who I was then (and I have no reason to assume she was lying when she said she didn't), then she certainly does now.

Before she knew who I am—how much money I'm worth—she was afraid of me. I unwittingly creeped her out, just like that girlfriend of my father's from all those years ago.

Maybe now that she knows I'm rich, she'll be nice to me. Ingratiating.

I don't know that I could handle that. Obviously, I shouldn't care one way or the other. By the time Thursday rolls around, I'm annoyed with myself. It's time to put an end to this shit.

So at six o'clock on Thursday evening, when Savannah shows up to make dinner, I am not up in my office, I'm sitting on one of the stools in the kitchen, answering emails on my laptop, music playing through my earbuds, like I own the place.

Which is my point.

I do own the place.

And that fact that I've been hiding from my personal chef for the past two months is ridiculous.

Still, I want the opportunity to look into her eyes and see whether my presence disturbs her.

What am I going to do if she is clearly still afraid of me?

I hate the idea of her working for me if she's afraid of me simply because she has no other options. No one should have to work in that environment.

I can't fire her. I know how desperately she needs this job.

That's when she walks in. I pretend not to hear the front door open, not to notice the way her steps slow as she reaches the kitchen and sees me there, as if she's debating what to do. I make a show of pulling out my earbuds and turning to glance over my shoulder.

Fuck, she's gorgeous.

Today she's not in the shorts and T-shirt she was wearing the other day.

Last night, a cold front came through. At least

what passes for a cold front in fall in Texas. Today the high was in the mid 70s. Practically sweater weather.

So today she's dressed in jeans and a T-shirt. It should be an improvement, because at least her legs aren't bare, but she's still barefoot. Her hair is up in another messy bun on top of her head. Her shirt looks to be a vintage Rolling Stones T-shirt. It's over-sized, the neck stretched out so that it hangs off one shoulder.

"I can leave and come back later."

Shit. I'm staring again.

Probably doing that thing where I don't blink often enough and wait too long to talk.

I drop my eyes to her feet. Because staring at someone's feet is less weird than staring at their shoulders?

Right?

Or is it weirder?

Why don't I know these things? These seemingly simple rules of how to interact with other people? Things everyone else seems to know instinctively.

"It's fine," she says.

Her tone is gentle, like she knows exactly what I'm thinking and how awkward I feel. Like she knows all of that, but that it really is fine.

I force myself to drag my gaze from her bare feet

up to her face. After all, that was the point, wasn't it? To look at her. Not to ogle her, but to figure out if she's freaked out by me.

So I give myself a second to do what I haven't done before. To really look at her face. Her lips are slightly parted and glistening. Her cheeks flushed—probably from carrying groceries over from her cottage. Her eyes are a striking blue, almost indigo. Her pupils dilated, likely because she just came inside from the outdoors and they are adjusting.

She looks gorgeous, surprised to find me here, but not afraid.

Her expression, much like her tone when she spoke, seems to indicate that everything is fine. That this is normal. That a boss who stares and talks in bursts and doesn't blink often enough is fine.

That I am fine just as I am. That I am not too weird. That I am not even a little bit scary.

Thank fuck.

I stand and move to pick up my laptop.

"I can move to my office."

She takes a hasty step forward. "You don't have to do that." She sets the bag down on the other side of the counter and starts unpacking it. "You're welcome to work in here while I cook. It's your house, after all."

"But it's your kitchen. I don't want to make you uncomfortable."

I'm watching her so closely I see the moment her gaze darts to mine, a frown of confusion flickering across your face.

"You don't." Her attention returns to the groceries as she clears her throat. "You don't make me uncomfortable."

I want to believe her, but I'm not sure I do. She doesn't seem to be lying, but I'm not good at catching lies when they're told by a beautiful woman. It's not one of my strong suits.

I'm about to make an excuse to leave, when she looks up at me again, and says, "Unless I make you uncomfortable. Don't feel like you have to stay and keep me company."

Well, fuck.

What am I supposed to do with that?

That's a hell of a question. No, she doesn't make me uncomfortable. At least not in the way she means it. But it's not like she makes me comfortable either. I'm not exactly relaxed. I'm far too alert for that. It's discomfort. But a discomfort, like I've never quite felt before. I feel alive and alert. The same way I do when I'm in the zone coding. Like I'm tapped into something bigger than myself.

"It's fine." She seems to take my words at face

value, nodding, as she washes produce. After a moment, she snaps open an earbud case and starts to put them in.

"You can connect to the Bluetooth speakers."

"The music won't bother you?"

"It won't." I know she likes to listen to music while she cooks. And that she taps into the speakers when I'm not here. She keeps the volume low, but sometimes when I'm up in my office and she's down here, bits of the music drift up from the stairs.

If I'm going to do this, I'm going to get the most out of it.

She connects her phone to the speakers and pulls up a playlist. It's a lot of female artists, most of them I've never heard of before.

So I stay, pretending to work on my laptop while she cooks, trying not to get turned on as she rubs oil on a whole chicken. There shouldn't be anything sexy about raw chicken. Of course, it's not the raw chicken that's doing it for me. It's her hands, strong and competent. It's the confidence with which she uses the tools at her disposal. Like the entire kitchen is an extension of her body.

Once the chicken is in the oven, she does a quick clean up before washing and drying her hands. She gets out more food—a bag of potatoes this time. She pulls out two potatoes and washes them before nudging the rest of the bag further down the counter. Then she pauses to pull out a protein bar and eats a bite before returning to peeling the potatoes.

She looks up to find me watching her. Her chewing slows as she brings her fingers up to brush away some crumbs.

"Sorry." She flashes me a sheepish grin. "I usually eat my dinner while I cook. If that bothers you, I can wait to eat after."

My gaze drops to the protein bar. "That's your dinner?"

"Yeah."

"You don't like roasted chicken?"

"I wouldn't make you something I didn't like." She shrugs. "Of course, I like most food if it's well prepared. And you haven't told me what you like, so I've been flying blind here." She tips her head to the side as she takes another bite for her bar, her tongue darting out to lick the crumbs off her lips. "Do you not like chicken? Because I can whip up something else."

"I love chicken," I snap, my response coming out too harsh, because the distraction of crumbs on her lips seems to be shutting down my central nervous system. "I just don't see why you're eating a protein bar for dinner when there's a whole chicken."

Her gaze shifts to the oven against the far wall and then back to me. "Oh." Then she chuckles, pointing at the oven. "That's your dinner. Not mine."

"You haven't been eating the food you prepare for me?"

"Of course not."

"Why not?"

"That's your food." She must see the source of my confusion, because she goes on. "I shop for you from a weekly budget Martin set up."

"Obviously," I snap, still not seeing her point.

"If I shopped for myself out of that budget, that would be stealing."

"No, it wouldn't," I argue automatically. "This weekly budget Martin gives you. Do you spend all the money every week?"

She seems to consider the matter for a moment, tipping her head to the side as if doing the mental math. I appreciate the way she's thinking about her answer almost as much as I appreciate the way her bun tips to one side as she does it.

Which is annoying. I should value honesty in an employee more than I value adorable head bobbling. I should not even notice the adorable things about her, but how can I not when there are so many?

After a moment she shakes her head. "No, I've

never spent all the money. But, to be fair, the budget Martin set is extravagant."

"Then you should use it to cover your own food as well."

"I can't do that," she says, with a patient smile.

"Why not?"

"Because I'm paid plenty of money. I can afford my own food."

I reach across the counter and pick up her discarded wrapper, flattening it smooth. "If you consider a store brand granola bar food."

She arches an eyebrow at me, her lip switching ever so slightly. I can't tell if I've amused her or annoyed her.

"As a matter of fact, I do consider it food."

"Well, I don't." A glance at the ingredient list tells me everything I need to know about this so called food she's eating.

"Since only one of us is a James Beard nominated chef, it's my opinion that matters."

I'm sure she thinks she's won the argument with that, but she clearly doesn't know how stubborn I can be.

"You're roasting an entire chicken," I point out.

She nods without glancing up from the potatoes she's peeling.

"Surely you don't expect me to eat the whole thing."

"Of course not. Chicken breast, pan drippings, mashed potatoes, and sautéed spinach for tonight. Tomorrow I'll be making chicken stock from the carcass and you'll be having chicken and spinach panini for lunch."

"Which still doesn't account for the whole bird."

She sighs. "Most of it though."

"Which means there should be plenty of chicken for both of us. There's no point in wasting food."

She looks up at me, squinting in a way that's challenging and a bit playful. "What are you, some sort of food waste expert?"

"It's an area of interest for me."

One of her eyebrows arches. "Really?"

Inspired, I type away on my keyboard, pull up the document I was reviewing last week, and then turn the laptop to face her.

She gives me the side eye before setting down her peeler and leaning over to squint at my computer screen. She plants her elbows on the counter, causing her shirt to gape, revealing the crest of her breasts.

Fuck me.

What is it about this woman that the barest hint of her tits gets me hard?

She reads the title of the article out loud. "The impact of food waste on global methane emissions by G. Mathews, et al." Then she straightens, rolling her eyes. "Seriously? You just have that at your fingertips?"

"I read it last week, actually."

She snorts. "Fine. I will eat some of the chicken."

I gesture to the bag of potatoes. "You'll have some of all of it."

She arches her eyebrow again, but pulls out a few more potatoes without comment.

A few minutes later, as she dices the potatoes and adds them to a pan with water, she asks, "So why the interest in food waste?"

"It was a source sited by a grant applicant."

"And you ..." She makes a tell-me-more gesture. "What? Just read grant applications in your spare time?"

"Actually, I read grant applications for my full-time job, now."

"So you're not just an eccentric, retired, billionaire entrepreneur?"

"Alas, not even a billionaire."

The noise she makes—halfway between a snort and scoff—says she doesn't believe me. I don't argue with her. After all, I'm plenty rich, even if my charitable donations keep me out of the billionaire club.

We keep chatting like this while she cooks. Eventually, she teases me into admitting how bored I was after I sold Cookie Jar. I didn't want to run the company anymore, but I didn't want to just do nothing. Eventually, a friend of a friend put me in contact with a non-profit that needed help reviewing grant proposals.

"What kind of grant proposals? Like, venture capital? What you'd see on Shark Tank?"

"No. Mostly for research grants."

She pauses while mincing garlic. "Like scientific research."

"Yes."

"And you just have a broad enough base of knowledge to review those?"

I shrug, remembering how annoyed Ava would get by all the reading I do. "I'm smart enough I can figure it out. I research anything I don't understand. And I'm only one person on a committee. If there's something I don't understand, I have backup."

Not that it's ever come to that.

Even though my background is in programming and finance, there's not much I can't learn if I put my mind to it.

She turns back to the oven, sautéing the spinach in silence for several moments. "So you're like, a legit genius then?"

What's the right answer here?

Ava hated how smart I was. Called me a snotty know-it-all.

Honestly, she's probably not wrong.

But I refuse to glorify ignorance. There's nothing sexy about stupidity.

And ... fuck ... it's not like it matters one way or the other if Savannah thinks I'm a know-it-all.

Because that's not what this is about. And what are we? Ten?

I huff out a breath, annoyed with myself for even hesitating to answer.

"Yeah. I guess I am."

I wait for some reaction from her. Some sign that she finds my overt nerdiness off-putting, but she says nothing.

I go back to my reading, not looking up again until I hear a pop followed by a sharp intake of breath.

I look up to see her standing on one foot, still facing the stove, rubbing the top of one foot against the denim covering her other calf.

"What happened?" I'm already on my feet and rounding the island.

"Nothing. Just splattered some grease."

She says "nothing" but I hear the strain in her voice.

I scoop her up and set her on the island, kneeling before her on one knee. I pull her foot onto my knee. A row of three bright red splotches dots the top of her foot.

"Ian! This isn't—"

"Why aren't you wearing shoes?"

"—necessary."

The sight of her delicate foot, of the angry-looking burns, sets my heart racing.

"Hey Siri, call 911," I bark. My phone, which is sitting out on the counter beside my laptop, stirs to life at the command.

She jerks her foot from my hand. "That's unnecessary."

Siri responds as well. "Calling emergency services in five seconds."

Savannah leans back, snatching up my phone and hitting the cancel button before Siri can make the call.

"You're hurt." Heart racing, I pull her foot back, cupping her heel, careful not to touch the burns.

"Not enough to call EMS." She leans over to point at the burns. "This is the only spot the grease splatter. Just the top of my foot."

"But—"

"Hey." She reaches down and cups my jaw, nudging my gaze up to hers. "I've been working in a kitchen more than half my life. I know how to treat burns. I know when they're serious and when they're not. If I needed EMS, I would let you call them. Trust me."

With her hands on my skin and her eyes meeting mine, the panic barreling through me slows down. But still ... that thought—the idea of her hurt and in pain... All the time, apparently—fills me with rage. It makes me want to destroy something in order to protect her. It makes me want to—

"Shhh..." she murmurs. "Trust me on this. This tiny burn is nothing. Look—" She lets go of my jaw to show me the inside of her upper arm where there's a round—ish scar about the size of a nickel.

I suck in a breath, at the sight of it.

"This was hot duck fat," she says with a nonchalant chuckle. "You don't even want to know how I got that one. Much worse than those tiny specks on my foot. And, look at these."

She hold out her hands, tracing scars along the back of her hands and her forearms. When I reach out and run a fingertip along an angled slash of a scar on her inner arm, she doesn't even flinch.

"These are all cuts. Most were minor. Oh, and look at this one. This was really bad." She pulls up the hem of her shirt to show off a swatch of her belly.

There's a blotchy burn scar a few inches from her belly button, but I can hardly see it because my vision is starting to tunnel from being so close to her. From having my hands on her skin and breathing in the scent of her.

And just like that, the rage turns to something else. Something that feels even more dangerous.

I don't just want to protect her. I want ... other things. Things I have no business wanting from this woman. Not when she's the most beautiful thing I've ever seen. Not when I'm her boss and she's completely at my mercy.

At my mercy, but in none of the ways I wish she was.

She studies my expression for a moment, her pupils dilated, her breathing shallow. "Trust me, okay? Chefs are tough. We're trained to be. It's fine. I'm fine."

Her touch, her words, her eyes staring into mine ... they all hypnotize me, and I feel myself nodding along with her.

I blow out a breath. "Okay. But you have to at least let me treat the burn."

"Okay." Lips twisting in a faint smile, she nods towards the range behind me. "But at least turn off the heat under the spinach. It's about a minute from being inedible."

I don't give a fuck about the spinach, but I follow her directions. I stand, reluctantly letting her foot drop from my hands as I turn to the range, cranking the knob to off and shifting the pan to the back burner.

"Hey, Siri, how do I treat a burn?"

Siri starts answering, but Savannah cuts her off. "Hey, Siri, stop."

I pick up her foot again, cradling it in my palm, and Savannah gives me a gentle kick with her other foot until I look at her again.

"A cool damp cloth will be fine."

"For how long?"

"Five or ten minutes. Tops."

It's my turn to arch a brow at her.

"Trust me," she says again.

Again, I want to argue, because a woman who accepted a job as a personal chef, living alone in the middle of nowhere with a strange man, can't actually be trusted to make sound decisions about her personal safety.

True, she probably knows more about how to treat burns than I do.

Reluctantly, I get out a clean towel, soak it with the cold water from the tap and bring it over to her. And instantly realize that unless I'm going to stand here holding her foot like a creeper, I won't be able to hold the towel in place.

So I pick her up and carry her around the island and set her down on a stool. I angle the other and prop up her foot before carefully draping the damp towel over it. Then I return with a dry towel to prop her foot up on.

She gives a huff of laughter. "Are you done?"

I look from her foot to her. "How does it feel?"

"It feels like you're being ridiculous."

"Why aren't you wearing shoes? Do you always cook barefoot? Because that can't be safe."

She bumps up her chin defiantly. "I can't just sit here. I need to check on the potatoes." She points across the kitchen. "They're going to boil over."

I look from her to the range, where it does, indeed, look like the potatoes are ... bubbly.

"Tell me what you need me to do." I point to her foot. "You, stay off your foot."

She looks like she wants to argue, but when I threaten to call 911 again, she talks me through checking them to see if they're done, draining them, and adding butter and some cream.

I stare into the pot. "How do I mash them?"

"You don't. I will. My ten minutes with a cool cloth is almost up."

Again, I want to argue with her. Even if this burn

isn't serious, there are a dozen other hot things in the kitchen. And sharp things.

"Cooking barefoot can't be safe," I grumble.

She shrugs. "I certainly wouldn't do it in a restaurant kitchen."

"Then why do you cook barefoot here?" Come to think of it, I've never seen her in shoes.

She looks pointedly at my own bare feet.

"What?" I blurt, not seeing the connection.

"You don't wear shoes in the house."

"So?"

"The first time I came here, I noticed you have a shelf for shoes by the front door. You don't wear shoes inside, so it's only polite that I don't wear them either."

I can feel my scowl deepening. That this is my fault, that she got hurt because of me, because she was trying to accommodate my idiosyncrasies, is enraging.

"You can wear shoes in the house," I tell her.

She smirks. "But you don't wear shoes in the house."

I don't.

And, no, I'm not a germaphobe. But I grew up around cattle and I've never gotten past how disgusting cow shit is on the bottom of your boots. Besides, if I wear shoes too long, my feet feel claustrophobic. Which is certainly not something I'm going to tell Savannah, since Ava laughed when I tried to explain it to her.

I wore shoes every day when I owned Cookie Jar.

If I don't have to wear them now that I'm working from home, I'm not going to.

"Just because I don't wear shoes in the house, that doesn't mean I want you cooking barefoot."

She holds up her hands like she's warding off my argument. "Hey, if me being barefoot in the kitchen bothers you, I can buy a pair of house shoes to wear in the kitchen."

"You doing something unsafe bothers me."

"This isn't a restaurant kitchen. There aren't fryers full of hot oil or people carrying knives around. Cooking barefoot in a home kitchen is pretty safe. Lots of people do it all the time."

I cross my arms over my chest. "It's not safe enough. I'll buy you a pair of shoes for the house. Just let me know what kind."

"I can buy my own shoes."

Great. The last thing she needs is to spend money she can't afford to waste buying shoes she wouldn't need if it weren't for my damn weird issues.

"You didn't buy pots and pans or knives when you started working here, did you?"

She looks like she's fighting a smile. "Actually, I did bring some of my own knives."

I pick up the vegetable peeler. "What about this? Or the colander? Or the range for that matter?"

She loses the fight with the smile.

Her grin just about guts me.

"I think you would have noticed if I'd hauled in my own six burner range."

"I'm your employer. It's my job to make sure you have the supplies you need to do your job. If that means shoes, then I can damn sure buy you shoes."

"Okay, okay."

"Pick out something and text me a link."

Twenty minutes later, a few bites into the most tender chicken I've ever eaten, an alert comes on my phone. It's a link to a pair of slip-on clogs with a note about her shoe size.

I look up at the woman sitting opposite me at the kitchen table. She smirks and gives a jaunty nod of her head.

She says nothing, but goes back to watching whatever is playing on her phone.

I click on the link which takes me to an online vender specializing in uniforms for chefs. The pair she picked out is ugly as fuck, on sale, and clearly the cheapest thing she could find. Obviously, I shouldn't have told her I'm not a billionaire.

When I was dating Ava, she'd coax me into going shopping with her. As if I didn't already know she was dating me for my money. I didn't give a fuck about Ava's feet, but spent a fortune on shoes for her.

Yet Savannah somehow thinks the best I can afford is a thirty-dollar pair of acid green crocs.

Later that night, I order her three pairs of shoes. One that's the pair she picked out and two more in similar styles, from top of the line brands.

I try not to worry about what will happen in the kitchen between now and when the shoes will arrive.

Just like I try not to worry about why I care this much about the safety of her feet.

texts between
savannah and
trinity
TENTH WEEK

Help!!!!

Trin???

I need advice!!!!

Are you there?

Hold your horses!

What's the big emergency???

Tonight I was making dinner for Ian and … things happened.

Things?

What things?

Tell me more!!!!

Well, for starters, he was there in the kitchen when I went over to cook.

And I offered to come back later. And he offered to leave.

But then he just ended up staying and we talked while I cooked.

Oh

You talked.

<GIF of clutching pearls>

Not talking!

Alert the town elders

Be patient

Oh, so you didn't just talk

Please tell me this story ends with you covered in whipped cream

Or him covered in whipped cream

Are you going to listen or not?

<GIF of a woman listening patiently>

Mostly, it was just us talking. About food and stuff.

Then he found out that I only cook for him, but eat like crap the rest of the time

You do eat like crap

I don't know how you're not worried about ruining your palate

Because my palate is fucking awesome, fuck you very much.

So, he insisted I eat with him.

Ah ... so it was like a date?

But you had to make the meal

That's not the weird part.

At some point, I burned my foot.

And he did this thing where he scooped me up and set me on the counter.

And he was holding my foot in his hand and treating my injury.

And it was super sexy and ... gah

<Gif of a woman throwing herself onto a bed>

And ... now you have a foot fetish?

Or you're worried he has a foot fetish?

Don't focus on the foot thing.

But foot stuff is super hot

I mean, with the right guy

Obviously.

But it just ... he was so intense.

And he wants to buy me shoes.

So he definitely has a foot fetish

No. Not like sexy shoes. Like, chef's shoes.

So that I won't be cooking barefoot.

What do you think that means?

Um ...

I don't know

What do you think it means?

I

Don't

Know

Okay then ...

What do you want it to mean?

I don't know that either.

Maybe you need to figure that out

You know what's weird, Trin?

What?

I felt really safe with him.

I mean, yeah, my foot hurt. And then on top of that, there were all the feelings.

All the you-want-to-get-him-naked feelings?

Just to be clear

Yes. All those feelings.

So there was all of that. But in addition to all of that, I just felt …

Safe.

Like he was going to take care of me.

And I've never felt that way with anyone else before.

Oh, baby girl … you've got it bad

That's what I'm afraid of.

How's the seduction going?

I hesitate to ask, but ... what seduction?

I thought we agreed you should seduce your hot, rich boss

No. You suggested I should sleep with him.

I told you it was a horrible idea.

Because you've decided he's not hot?

Because he's my boss.

Technically, weren't you Dan's boss?

Right. Because that turned out so well.

Well, it would have turned out better if Dan was as hot as Ian Donavon and even half as rich

Let's not focus on the money stuff.

It makes me uncomfortable.

Why?

Has he bought you a pair of Louboutin heels to wear while cooking?

Something else expensive, then?

Not really.

Wait. What does that mean?

Has he bought you anything else or not?

He bought a big TV and had it installed in the kitchen.

Connect the dots for me

Did he buy it so you could watch TV while you cook?

Because that's not really your thing. You listen to music while you cook

The TV showed up the day after we ate dinner together.

That first night, I watched an episode of Brooklyn Nine-Nine on my phone while I ate.

Best show ever

Agreed.

And then the next day, there's this TV in the kitchen. And soon as I plate the food, he turns it on and cues up Brooklyn Nine-Nine.

Which I don't think he'd ever even watched before, because he kept asking questions about the characters.

So you think he bought the TV so you'd have things to watch while you eat?

I think he's into you

I just don't know.

You know how you can find out?

Tonight, just go in there and strip naked

I'm not having this conversation with you.

When did you get so boring?

When did you get so pervy?

This from the woman who introduced me to Dramione fanfic

Hey, what happens on my kindle, stays on my kindle.

Does that mean there's some super sexy hot-boss romances on your kindle?

Just stop it.

Okay?

Why?

Because Ian is a genuinely nice guy and he doesn't deserve to have you objectifying him like this.

OMG

What?

Oh

My

God

You like him!

Shut up.

You.

Like.

Him.

Like, like him, like him.

Are you having a stroke?

That's what she said!

<GIF of Michael Scott>

I'm serious.

You need to stop this right now.

Okay, all joking aside…

Are you going to …

What?

Am I going to what?

Make your move?

Again, and for the last time, I am not having this conversation with you.

Just hear me out … Dan was an asshole

Everyone who ever met him thought you could do better

I'm not sure I see where you are going with this.

Because from where I'm standing, it just sounds like you're insulting me.

No, I'm insulting Dan. And maybe your taste in men

But my point is this: you deserve better than Dan. And now, you're practically living with this guy who is rich and hot and clearly into you and everything you deserve in a guy

He's not.

What?

He's not into me.

What?

Why wouldn't he be into you?

I thought he bought you shoes? And a TV? And was all super protective of you?

Yeah. He did.

And he was.

But he hasn't made a move.

Like, at all.

Define "at all"

He hasn't so much as touched me
since the whole foot burn incident.

Not at all?

Not at all.

No moves have been made.

Huh

The way you described him cradling
your foot just seemed …

Really hot?

Exactly

Really hot

But nothing since then?

Nothing.

Not a single touch.

Huh

Idk

Maybe he was just really worried I'd
sue for negligence

Or whatever people sue for when they get hurt on rich people's property

That doesn't sound like something he'd be worried about

I think we need to both stop pretending we know him better than we do.

Because obviously, we don't know him.

And if he was into me, he would have made some kind of move by now.

But like … are you still eating meals with him?

Twice a day.

And you just … what?

Sometimes we watch TV while we eat. Sometimes we talk.

What do you talk about?

Recipes I've been trying. Or working on. Places I've traveled.

Sometimes he tells me about the research he's doing.

About the projects he's studying.

Trin, you would not believe how smart this guy is.

It's crazy how much he knows about so many different topics.

It's just ...

And you just talk?

He never tries to ... you know...

Nope.

It doesn't make sense. Men only talk to women they're into

And they really only listen to women they're into

I think maybe he's just lonely.

You know what I think?

I never know what you think.

And I'm not even sure I want to.

I think that if he's not into you, then he's not as smart as you think he is

How is it going?

Any movement on the seduction front?

Any more fancy gadgets show up?

Helloooooooo

Are you even there?

Have you blocked me?

Where

Are

You????

Have you been abducted by aliens?

Sa

Van

Ahhhhhhhh

Okay. I'm getting really worried.

I called and you didn't answer.

Are you okay?

Fuck.

I overslept.

How is it almost noon?

Dare I hope you overslept because you finally jumped your hot boss?

What? No response?

<GIF of a crickets chirping>

SAVANNAH

Answer me damn it!

Sorry.

I feel like shit

Hungover feel like shit or something else?

You poor baby

Do you need me to bring you soup?

No. I'll be fine.

But ... fuck.

I need to text Ian and let him know I can't cook for him today.

Hey, boss.

I'm not feeling well.

I won't make it down to make you lunch but I can talk you through some meals I have in the freezer for you.

Sorry I didn't make it down to make you breakfast.

Don't worry about breakfast.

What are your symptoms?

Nothing too scary.

I should be back up and running by tomorrow

Or maybe the day after

Fever?

Chills?

Nausea?

Savannah?

Induce

Bo

Wait stupid

Autocorrect g

I'm dine

I'm coming up.

I have a key and will let myself in.

I'm fine.

You don't need to come up.

This is nonnegotiable.

I only mentioned it so you wouldn't
worry when I let myself in.

ten

SAVANNAH

I don't know how much time passes between when I texted Ian and I hear him moving around the kitchen.

Mr. Sniggles is curled up beside me. Thank God.

He must be snuggling for warmth, because it's freezing in here.

Did another cold front come through?

I drift back to sleep before I can go find Ian and ask him to turn on the heat in the cottage before he goes back to the main house.

The next time I wake up, it's later in the day. I can tell because the door to the bedroom is open now and from my spot on the bed, I can see straight through the living area to the tiny kitchen at the front of the cottage.

Ian is standing at the sink, looking out the window as he talks on the phone. The sunlight shining in surrounds him like a halo. I can barely make out his side of the conversation as he gives the person on the other end of the phone his address. Mr. Sniggles sits at Ian's feet pawing at Ian's leg.

Ian absentmindedly reaches down and scratches Mr. Sniggles's huge fluffy head.

I hope he figures out that Mr. Sniggles is begging for food.

When I wake the next time, Ian is standing beside my bed, talking to a man I've never seen before. He's holding my cat.

I got Mr. Sniggles from a local rescue place a couple of years ago. Based on his size and general temperament, I think he's a Maine Coone—Mantee mix. He's huge and timid and hides from everyone but me. And apparently Ian.

"Mr. Sniggles doesn't like to be held," I mutter, sounding sleepy and grumpy and out of sorts.

Both men and the cat all turn toward me at the sound of my voice. I swear Mr. Sniggles huffs in indignation.

"Ah! You're awake," the stranger says, stepping closer and sitting on the edge of the bed. He runs a hand over my forehead. "Do you think you can sit up? I'd like to take your temperature and listen to your lungs."

"Of course I can sit up." Though when I try to get my hands under me and push up, I'm far weaker than I should be. "Who are you? How long was I asleep?" I glare at Ian and Mr. Sniggles. "Why are you holding my cat?"

Ian answers first. "He seems to like it."

He rounds to the other side of the bed, sets Mr. Sniggles by my feet, and reaches across to effortlessly hoist me into a sitting position.

"I had it," I grumble in protest.

Ian smirks. "Of course you did."

My cat paws at him, and he drops his hand back to Mr. Sniggles's head.

"I'm Dr. Berry," the other man says, answering the question I'd almost forgotten I'd asked. "Mr. Donavon here called and asked me to have a look at you."

"Oh. That's not necessary."

"I agree." The doctor runs his hands over my throat, palpating my lymph nodes. "I think it's probably just a bad cold. But I'll test you for the flu, covid, and strep, just to be sure."

He whips out an old-fashioned thermometer from a pocket and pokes it in my mouth, rambling about how he prefers this kind to the new-fangled ones as he presses a stethoscope to my chest and tells me to take a breath.

Even as sleep befuddled and groggy as I am, I know three things:

1. Doctors who make house calls are hella expensive.

2. I definitely can't afford this.

3. Ian is clearly some kind of cat whisperer

Nearly an hour later, I've been tested and cleared of the flu, covid, and strep. I've been ordered to rest, hydrate, and take over the counter pain meds as needed. The doctor gave me samples for a heavy duty cough medicine, along with a prescription that someone will deliver out to the house. And I have a written prescription (I'm not making this up) "At least three days of TLC."

I try to roll my eyes and make a snarky comment about it, but the hour of sitting up in bed, answering questions, and being poked and prodded by test swabs has worn me out. The hard-core cough medicine Ian poured down my throat probably helped. I'm asleep again before Dr. Berry even leaves.

texts between ian and martin

TWELFTH WEEK

Do I have control issues?

Obviously.

This is just occurring to you
only now?

Apparently.

Let me rephrase.

Why is this occurring to you now?

Savannah is sick. I don't like it.

First off, calm down. It's probably
not contagious.

Also, how do you know she's sick?
Did you hear her sneeze? Cedar
pollen counts are off the map this
year. Everyone has cedar fever.

And if you're looking for a reason to fire her, that one won't do.

But if you're worried about germs, give her a couple of days off to get over it.

Fuck off.

And no I'm not trying to fire her because she has cedar fever.

How much of an asshole do you think I am?

A total asshole. I thought we had established that.

Savannah is sick. I called the doctor, he tested for flu, covid, and strep. They all came back negative. He thinks it's just a virus.

WTF?

You called a doctor? Because she's feeling sick?

Obviously.

One of those places that does house calls?

Obviously.

How did you even know she was sick?

She texted and said she couldn't come down to cook for me.

I went out to the cottage to check on her, and she was feverish. So I called the doctor.

I'm not a complete asshole, despite what some people apparently think.

I was texting for advice, because I don't know what else I should do.

Like, legally?

You want to know what else you need to do legally so that she can't sue you for negligence or whatever?

No.

I don't know what I else I should do to help her feel better.

Do you have any suggestions or not?

I'm going to need a minute here.

I'm just surprised.

Why?

Clearly, you have forgotten that time in college when we were rooming together and I had the flu.

I haven't forgotten. You threw up all over the bathroom.

Yeah. And I passed out on the floor on my way back to the bed. You stepped over me on your way out the door to class.

It was the week of finals. I couldn't miss class because you were sick.

This woman has seriously gotten under your skin?

Fuck off

Should I start working on your prenup now?

Fuck

Off

Dude, I'm just saying...

I've never seen you like this before.

Not over a woman.

Not over anything that wasn't Cookie Jar.

What? Now you're ignoring me?

Super fucking mature, buddy.

She doesn't feel that way about me.

You are clearly head over heels for this chick.

Which means jack shit since she doesn't feel the same way

Has she said that out loud? Have you asked her?

No.

I'm her boss. I can't make a move on her.

Technically, I'm her boss.

As long as I don't make a move on her, we're okay.

What?

No response?

It was a joke.

Not a funny one.

You're the one who keeps telling me how much she needs the money.

Yeah. She needs the money. Have you asked her about that yet?

No. Because it wouldn't be appropriate.

Jesus.

Get your head out of your ass and talk to the woman.

Have an actual fucking conversation with her.

Because there are a whole host of fucking financial problems that will go away if she marries you.

I can't tell if that's a suggestion or a warning.

I guess it's both.

?

Don't take this the wrong way

?

You don't have a lot of experience with women

Why would I take that the wrong way?

It's a statement of fact.

Right. What was I thinking?

My point is this

As far as I know, your first serious relationship was with Ava. Correct?

Correct

So, basically, you were a 29 year old billionaire before you had your first girlfriend.

That's an exaggeration.

?

I'm not a billionaire

That's not the point. You're fucking rich as fucking hell.

And Ava was your first serious relationship. And it didn't exactly end well. And now you're head over ass for Savannah. Who you barely know.

So, yeah.

I'm worried this is going to end badly for you.

Okay, did I piss you off again? Because you've gone silent again.

Just thinking.

This situation is nothing like what happened with Ava.

Because Savannah Is your employee?

Because I know how this is going to end.

Okay. How is it going to end?

The way it was always meant to end. When the year of her employment is up, she's going to get that big bonus you promised her. And she's going to walk away.

This situation isn't different because she's my employee. It's different because I'm her boss.

Setting aside the fact that you're not her boss, I'm not sure I see the difference.

The difference is, she doesn't see me as anything other than her employer.

Yeah, you keep saying that. But unless you talk to her, you don't know that for sure.

SAVANNAH

I dream I'm in a boat, curled up asleep on one of the cushioned seats in the back while my grandpa fishes off the front, like I used to do when I was little. I would beg him to take me fishing and then get bored and fall asleep, lulled by the gentle rocking of the boat.

This time when I wake up, I feel better. Slightly.

My chills have passed, probably due to the Tylenol, the cough medicine, and the tea Ian forced down me during the doctor's visit.

When I reach out to pat the bed, I can feel Mr. Sniggles curled up beside me. He purrs the second I pet him—despite being a heartless traitor.

"Don't think I don't remember your betrayal," I mutter to him. "And while I was defenseless no less."

"You can't blame him. He was hungry," a sleepy voice says from the darkness.

I sit up, my head still spinning a little. "Ian?"

"Yeah?"

That's when I realize I'm not in my own bed. The bed in the cottage is a full. Comfortable. Fine. But nothing special.

The bed I'm in now is a vast, cloud-like expanse of fine-spun cotton that smells faintly of cedar and ... "Is this a weighted blanket?"

A light flicks on from the bedside table to reveal Ian sitting in a chair beside the bed.

The room is huge and sparsely decorated in the same sleek, mid-century modern lines as the rest of the house. It's too big to be a guest room, so it must be Ian's room. Which means I'm in his bed.

"Yeah," he says, his gaze roaming over my face like he's searching for an answer to a question he hasn't yet asked. "I hope it's okay that I put it on you. Some people find them claustrophobic."

Okay? No. It's more than okay. It's amazing. Like being hugged by the bed.

"Yes," I murmur, my voice rough with sleep. I swallow, wincing at how raw my throat feels.

The discomfort brings everything else into sharper relief. I'm in Ian's bed. What the hell?

I sit bolt upright. Or rather, I try to sit bolt upright. That's my instinct, at least.

Between the weight of the blanket, Mr. Sniggles, and my general fuzzy headedness, I don't sit bolt upright so much as flail around, like some sort of infant. Eventually, I shove the blanket off enough to angle my upper body off the bed. I look around, taking in my surroundings.

The room is dimly lit by a shaft of light pouring in from an open doorway through which I see a slice of cool white tile. The bathroom then. There's another doorway and another light on, on the far side of the room. Ian was seated in the chair a few feet from the bed, but when I started to flail around, he came to stand beside the bed. "What do you need?"

"This is your bedroom."

"Yes."

"Why am I in your bedroom? What the hell happened?" I swallow again, wincing again. Fuck, I hate having a sore throat.

Instead of answering my questions, Ian grabs some pillows and slides them behind my back. It's all very Florence Nightingale for someone that the internet claims has circuit boards in place of a heart.

And yes, ever since he gave me permission to google him, I've been shamelessly reading everything my iPhone can get its greedy little paws on.

Don't judge me.

"I don't understand what's happening here. How did I get here?"

His blank look implies it's a stupid question. "I carried you."

"Why?"

"The doctor said you needed someone to watch over you. It seemed logical that it would be easier to do it from here than in the cottage. The sofa in the cottage proved..." He trails off as if searching for the right word. "Incompatible with getting a good night's sleep."

"Wait. You slept on my sofa?"

His lips twist in either a grimace or an attempt at a smirk. "Not very well."

A series of images parade through my imagination. First, his tall frame draped over the loveseat in the cottage, head angled awkwardly on one arm, his legs draped over the other like a cartoon.

I wouldn't be able to sleep on the loveseat even if I curled into a fetal position, so there's no way he could.

The second image that pops into my mind is less comical. It's of him carrying me, bride-style down to the house. Is that why I dreamed of sleeping in my grandpa's boat? Of the gentle rocking? And the feeling of being completely safe?

Why do I feel so safe around this man? This man I barely know?

"You carried me down to your house and I didn't even wake up?" I ask, even though that must be what happened. Unless Ian has secretly been developing transporter technology.

"Obviously." He gives a tight nod. "You seemed to drift in and out."

"What was *in* that cough medicine?"

"I believe it's a mixture of—"

"That was a rhetorical question."

"Oh."

I'm still struggling to process all of this when Mr. Sniggles bumps his head against my hand in an obvious bid for attention.

"And you brought Mr. Sniggles, too?"

"Obviously."

I mentally roll my eyes at myself. What is up with all the stupid questions? Yes, I'm sick, but is this virus eating my brain?

Obviously, Ian must have brought Mr. Sniggles. It's not like Mr. Sniggles could have ventured out of the cottage on his own to search for me Incredible-Journey style.

But at the same time ... the idea that my aloof employer is taking such good care of me, that he not only carried me down to his house so I could sleep in his bed, but that he also brought my cat?

It's all so improbable.

People don't do this kind of thing.

No one I know has ever taken care of me like this. Not since I was a child.

Yes, my mom cared for me when I was sick as a child, obviously. But even then, I was a stubborn little brat who didn't like to accept help from anyone.

"He needs food. And water. And a litter box."

Ian arches an eyebrow. "Obviously. Clearly, the fact that you feed me three meals a day has given you the impression that I'm unable to care for myself, let alone another creature. Nevertheless, I assessed his needs and brought all of those things down to the house."

His stoic delivery leaves acres of territory for a smart-ass comeback, but I'm too tired to think of one. Instead, I sink back against the pillows, let my eyes flutter closed, and take comfort in the low rumble of Mr. Sniggles's purring and the delightful weight of the blanket.

The scent of cedar and bergamot provides another layer of comfort.

"While you're awake, try to drink some broth. You need as many fluids as you can take."

"There should be some broth in the—"

"I already heated it up."

Ian moves to sit on the bed, holding out an insulated mug with a straw. I take a sip of my homemade chicken broth, warmed to the perfect temperature.

I take a few more sips of broth, then comment, "You'll be sorry later when you don't get chicken and dumplings next week."

"I'll live."

Even the minor effort of sitting up in bed tires me out way more quickly than it should. After a few moments, I feel myself drifting back to sleep. I curl over onto my side, facing his chair. The last thing I think is that I am the one who is supposed to be taking care of him, not the other way around.

twelve

IAN

Obviously, texting Martin for advice was a bad idea. When another day passes and Savannah still isn't feeling better, I'm out of ideas. Unfortunately, the internet isn't much more help. After thirty minutes of research online, I have to talk myself out of driving her into town to one of those clinics that does a full body scan. Surely, if Dr. Berry thought this was a cancer, he would have suggested something other than Tylenol, fluids, and rest.

I'm almost tempted to call my mom and ask her for advice. Unfortunately, she's in Spain right now and it's the middle of the night. If she's awake at three in the morning, I don't want to know what she's doing.

In lieu of doing something that might actually be helpful, I simply sit by her bedside in a chair I dragged up from my office. At some point, I get up to take a phone call from my assistant. When I return, Mr. Sniggles is sitting in the chair I vacated.

"I was sitting there."

His only response is a dismissive slow blink.

So I go back to my office for a second chair.

He and I sit there at her bedside in silence for long enough that I lose track of time.

I'm nearly asleep sitting up when she coughs and rolls over.

Mr. Sniggles sits up, suddenly alert and glares at me.

"I know it sounds bad. But you heard the doctor. It's just a virus. And according to Harvard Health, most colds have a lingering cough."

Mr. Sniggles does not look impressed.

"Do you have any other suggestions?"

He gives me another slow blink.

"Yeah. I didn't think so. You are about as helpful as Martin was."

Though, at least Mr. Sniggles can't voice any opinions about Ava.

I don't need Martin to tell me this is a shit show.

Just like I don't need Martin to warn me about getting too attached to Savannah. Martin should know better than anyone that attachment isn't really my thing.

At least, it never has been before now.

thirteen

SAVANNAH

The next couple of days pass in a blur.

Every time I wake, Ian is either by my side or close enough that I can hear him talking. He plies me with a steady stream of warm broth, hot tea and whatever medications the doctor left for me. There's Tylenol for the pain and cough medicine that helps me sleep. Thank God, I am strong enough to stand and make it to the bathroom, because I don't think I could've handled the humiliation of having him help me do that.

Sometimes when I wake up, I hear him talking on the phone in the hall just outside the bedroom, his deep voice a comforting rumble as he talks about finances and proposals, throwing around scientific terms I don't understand. Other times, I wake to find him reading in the chair by my side. Inevitably, he sets aside his work, and turns on the TV to watch an episode of Brooklyn Nine-Nine with me. I'm too tired to stay awake for long and there's something oddly comforting about falling asleep to the sound of his gentle laughter.

When I wake up on the morning of what I think is the third day, I feel almost human. My fever broke in the night and when I swallow it no longer feels like I've been gargling battery acid.

On the downside, I feel good enough to recognize how gross I feel. My skin is sticky, my teeth are gritty, and I undoubtedly stink. I need a shower so badly my hair hurts.

I get up to pee, fully intending to go all the way back to my cottage to shower, but the trek to the toilet is enough to leave me winded.

Even if Ian volunteered to carry me back to my cottage, there's no way I'd let anyone touch me when I smell like this. I tuck my nose into the collar of my T-shirt and give a sniff.

Yep. This is why medieval Europeans thought the plague was spread by smell alone.

From beyond the open door of the bedroom, I

can hear the murmur of Ian on the phone and decide to take matters into my own hands.

I sneak into the bathroom and crank on the shower.

Is it weird to shower in someone's bathroom? Possibly.

But, I've been sleeping in his bed and peeing in his toilet for days now, so this isn't any weirder than that. I just hope the shower revives me enough that I have the energy to put fresh sheets on his bed, because he has already gone above and beyond in caring for me.

I'm already in the shower when there's a knock on the door.

"Yeah?"

The glass encased shower isn't directly in the line of sight of the door, but there are mirrors scattered around the room, so I can see the reflection of the door cracking open.

Ian barely opens the door and calls through the gap. "You're showering?"

I feel well enough to smirk as I parrot his standard answer. "Obviously."

There's an awkward beat before he asks, "Do you need any help?" He clears his throat and then adds in a rush, "Not in a creepy way. Just because you've been sick."

"No. I've got this." But thanks for driving home how unappealing you find me.

Though to be fair, no one is at their sexiest when they've been sick.

"Are you sure? It doesn't seem safe. The last time you were up, you could barely stand on your own."

"I am fine. I promise." It's a little weird talking to him while I shower. There's an intimacy to it, what with me being naked and this space being so much his. I don't let myself think about it too long because it feels like dangerous ground. Like territory he wouldn't want my mind tromping around in.

So I push the thought aside and squirt a dollop of shampoo from a fancy-looking bottle into my palm. It smells like him. Woodsy, like cedar and moss, and masculine. "I promise I'll sit down if I feel lightheaded."

"That's less reassuring than you think."

"I'm almost done, anyway."

"Do you even have clothes to change into?"

I pause while rinsing my hair. Clearly, I did not think this through.

In my haste to get in the shower and de-gunk my hair, I didn't think as far as clothes. "I guess I'll just put on what I had."

Yep, that's gross, but not as gross as my hair was five minutes ago.

"My closet opens into the bathroom. Help your-self to a T-shirt and sweats or whatever."

"Thank you."

A moment later, I hear the door close again. I rinse my hair and give my body a final scrub.

When I'm done with the shower, I wrap myself in a huge, fluffy towel, then I pad barefoot over to the door at the end of the room that must open into his closet.

His closet is as expensive and luxurious as I would've expected. There's a section of suits and business attire, even though I've never seen him dressed in anything other than sweats and T-shirts. Another row of less formal clothing, that, again, he doesn't wear. The opposite wall has a built-in dresser and shelving. That's where I find the sweats and T-shirts that are so familiar.

Since I don't have clean underwear to change into, I go commando as I pull on a pair of oversized sweats and a T-shirt. Yep. Commando in my boss's pants. Bold move, right?

Is it weird to have all my intimate bits naked against his clothes? Maybe. Probably.

But it doesn't feel weird. It feels intimate and licentious. Delicious and illicit. I'm certainly not underweight, but I'm shorter than he is, and his clothes seem to swallow me whole. Still, there's something comfortable about the worn cotton.

Even though it's just sweats and a T-shirt, I'm sure they're the rich person version of these basic items. I bet they're woven from organic cotton and silk from free-range butterflies or some such nonsense. My point is this: everything touching my skin is luxurious, soft, and touchable. Wrapping myself in layers of Ian feels like the most decadent thing I've ever done.

There's a wallet sitting out on top of the dresser. Obviously, I don't dig through it, but I let my fingers linger over the soft leather. There's also a T-shirt draped casually over the edge, like he pulled it off and dropped it there. My virus is clearly still affecting my brain function, because I can't resist picking it up and holding it to my nose, huffing in the scent of him like a drug addict.

Would he notice if I stole it? Probably. I'm tempted to replace it with the one I'm wearing so that I can walk around covered in his scent, but that seems too self-indulgent even for me.

I give the closet one last look. He's so quiet and self-contained. Somehow the closet says things he won't. As many clothes as he has, they barely take up a third of the space. This isn't a house design for a single man. And somehow the emptiness of the closet makes me feel a little sad.

Partly for him, because the unused space in the closet seems lonely. When Ian bought this house, did he imagine his ex living here with him? Did he think her expensive clothes would hang beside his, taking up all that extra room? Does he feel sad every time he comes in here, faced with a reminder of the relationship he doesn't have?

It makes me feel sad, but something else as well. Something even less pleasant. Defensive, maybe? Angry on his behalf. Offended that dumb bitch didn't see what she had. Maybe even a little righteous on his behalf. If she didn't have the good sense to hold onto him while she had him, she doesn't deserve him.

He deserves someone who sees how wonderful he is. How kind and thoughtful. He deserves someone...

My thoughts stutter to a halt.

I need to rein myself back in. He might deserve better than her, but that doesn't mean I deserve him.

fourteen

IAN

Six months ago, I would've described myself as a simple man with simple needs. All I wanted was to live alone and do my work in peace.

Now, all of that has changed.

Now the most beautiful woman I've ever seen is showering in my bathroom, and I can't get the image of her naked, wet body out of my mind.

No, I didn't intend to sneak a peek at her like a goddamn pervert. I cracked open the door just to make sure she was okay and hadn't fallen or something. I purposefully kept my gaze away from the shower. Unfortunately, there are too damn many reflective surfaces in my bathroom, one of which gave me a perfect view of her body as she scrubbed shampoo into her hair. And like a damn creep, I just stood there, watching the water sluice over her body.

Thank god she didn't catch me acting like a pervert.

Part of me wants to jump in the car, drive away and never come back to this house. Part of me wants to go into the hall bathroom and jerk off so that at least I can relieve some of the pressure. Of course, the largest part of me wants to go back upstairs to the bedroom and join her in the shower.

Not that I'm going to do any of those things.

She's been sick. She's at my mercy and in my care. I'm her boss, for Christ's sake. Even if I wasn't her boss, joining her in the shower would be out of the question. See the above. She's been sick, and she's in my house under my protection. She didn't choose to come here on her own. I carried her here while she was too sick to protest.

Mere minutes ago, I was afraid she wouldn't be strong enough to stand up in the shower. She certainly wouldn't be strong enough for me to fuck her up against the wall.

Since I can't fuck her and I can't abandon her, I do the next best thing. I make her dinner.

Or at least I try to.

I've worked my way through all the broth she had stashed in the freezer. There are a bunch of ingredients in the refrigerator, but I can't cook. If I could, I wouldn't have ended up in this place to begin with. Which leaves me with the options that I had before Martin hired her. Pizza seems out of the question since she's been on a liquid diet for the past three days. So I call up the Chinese-Mexican restaurant, order two different soups, and promise to tip the guy fifty bucks if he can get it here to me in twenty minutes.

Which leaves me twenty minutes to figure out how to erase the image of her from my mind before I have to go back up there and face her again.

I'm still pacing the kitchen, wondering what I'm supposed to do when her cat emerges from the stairs to stand in the doorway and meows at me.

The innocuously named Mr. Sniggles is a long-haired beast of a cat who weights at least thirty pounds and I suspect is part bobcat. He has long fur and a noticeable crick in his tail. One of his eyes looks a little squinty, as if he got into a barroom brawl once, and it never quite recovered. Despite his size and his bad ass attitude, his meow, which I hadn't heard until now, is surprisingly high-pitched. I look at him in surprise because he hasn't sought me out before now. "What do you want?"

He gives me a slow blink and then meows again.

"Your food and water are upstairs," I remind him.

Another slow blink. Another meow. Then he turns and heads up the stairs. When I don't follow, he meows again just out of sight, but close enough to make his point.

"All right, all right. I'm coming."

I find Savannah about halfway down the stairs sitting, with her head resting on her arms, which are folded on her knees. Mr. Sniggles gives me a look as soon as she comes into view, as if to say, "See? This is what I was trying to tell you."

"Savannah, are you okay?"

By the time I reach her, she's sitting up, a sheepish smile playing at her lips.

"I really felt strong enough to make it downstairs. Just got a little lightheaded, but I'm fine."

"You should've waited for me."

She waves a hand as if to wipe away my irritation. "Settle down, I'm fine."

"You're not fine. You can't even make it down the stairs. You should've waited." I know I sound like an asshole, but I'm not mad at her. I'm mad at myself. I shouldn't have left her alone.

Worse still, the only reason she was alone is

because I didn't trust myself to be there in the other room while she was showering.

She stands up, wobbling slightly on her feet before I steady her with a hand on her shoulder. "I shouldn't have left you by yourself. Let me get you back upstairs."

"No, I've been in that room too long. Bring me downstairs, if you insist on carrying me."

"I do."

I sweep her up into my arms just like I did when I carried her down to the house three days ago. It's different now though. She's clean and awake and her hair smells slightly of my shampoo.

Seeing her dressed in my clothes, smelling the scent of my soap and shampoo on her skin and hair, stirs some kind of caveman response within me I never could've anticipated. Makes me want to keep her in my bedroom forever, burn the rest of her clothes and insist that from now on she only wear things that I've worn first.

"You're going to have to fumigate your bedroom or something. It smells like a hospital ward in there." She wrinkles her nose, giving her head a little shake, that I feel rather than see because it causes her cheek to brush against my chest. "No, not a hospital ward. That would smell like bleach and cleaner. This just smells like a sweaty, sick person. I'm sorry."

"Don't worry about it."

"I tried to change your sheets myself. I only got as far as pulling off the blanket, though."

"I'll take care of it."

What I want to say is *I'll take care of you.*

Which is baffling, because even if she wanted that (and she probably doesn't), what do I actually know about taking care of another person?

I can start a business. I can earn millions of dollars. I can read scientific journal articles on unfamiliar topics and then deep dive on the research until the material is familiar.

Anything scientific, engineering, or math related, I can learn. Some of it comes easily to me. Some of it doesn't. But I can do it.

But personal stuff? Human interaction stuff? All of that is so much harder.

When I was a kid, my mom made me a damn chore chart for how to be a member of the family. She gave me a star every time I remembered to ask someone how their day was, for fuck's sake.

So, do I know how to take care of Savannah?

No. Not even a little.

But Martin said I could learn. If I wanted to. Maybe he's right. If I can learn enough about microbiology to have an opinion on what research is worth funding, then maybe I can learn this.

Even more surprising, I want to.

At least I want to try.

If the past three days have taught me anything, it's that.

Six months ago, I was perfectly happy being alone. Now ... now that I've sat by Savannah's bedside while she was sick, now that I've carried her in my arms, now that she's been naked in my shower and smells like my soap, I don't want to be alone anymore.

fifteen

SAVANNAH

For a guy who can barely keep himself fed, Ian makes an excellent caretaker.

Okay, so I don't know that he can barely keep himself fed. But I'm assuming, since Martin had to hire me to cook for him, that Ian wasn't doing a great job feeding himself before I came along.

After my embarrassing display of inferior lung capacity on the stairs ...

And can we just talk about how humiliating *that* was? Who can't walk downstairs on their own? Who?

Anywho...

After my embarrassing display of weakness, Ian

gets me settled on the sofa and cues up an episode of Brooklyn Nine-Nine. He spends an inordinate amount of time fussing with pillows and a blanket, fluffing and then stepping back to study the effect, as if my comfort is a complex scientific mystery he needs to unravel.

Is he hoping to win the Nobel Prize for pillow fluffing? Or maybe he's worried I'm going to file a workman's comp complaint?

At some point, I feign sleep just so he'll give it a rest. And because I have the energy levels of a newborn kangaroo, I actually fall asleep.

When I wake up, there's a tray of food on the coffee table. There's a travel mug with warm herbal tea, along with a to-go container of soup. The soup seems to be chicken tortilla soup, but with wontons. A weird combo for sure, but unexpectedly good.

I can hear Ian on the phone in the other room, undoubtedly on one of his many business phone calls. This one is something about the acidification of oceans, kelp forests, and mussels. For a guy who claims to be retired, he puts in some long hours.

As soon as I sit up, I notice Ian has gone silent, usually a sign his call has ended. I look up in time to see him propping his shoulder against the doorway between the kitchen and the living area.

"You're up." He tucks his phone in his pocket as he walks towards me. "How's the soup?"

"Weird." I tuck myself in the sofa's corner, leaving him plenty of room to sit. "But somehow, not as weird as it should be."

He chuckles, sitting at the other end of the sofa. Despite the size of the room, the sofa is a simple, sleek black leather sofa, so he's not that far away. "Yeah, no one ever expects Tortilla Wonton Soup to be good, but it is."

"I guess better this than the Spanish Inquisition," I quip, slurping up a wonton.

He tips his head, frowning.

I laugh at his obvious confusion. "Come on. Monty Python? 'No one ever expects the Spanish Inquisition'? Don't tell me you've never seen it."

"I've never seen any Monty Python."

"No way!" I reach out a foot to nudge his leg, sure he's teasing me.

He just shrugs. "Why would I have? Wasn't that show from the sixties?"

"Um ... the seventies. And it was a show and there were movies. Besides, you're a geek. I thought all geeks were Monty Python fans."

He squirms, swallowing visibly. "First off, most people would consider me a nerd, not a geek."

"Oh, my gosh. You're blushing." I give his leg

another playful nudge. "Are you seriously embarrassed by this?" He scowls and I can't tell if he's legitimately annoyed or just messing with me. I hold up a hand in truce. "Okay, okay. I'll stop teasing you, but first you have to explain what the difference is between a nerd and a geek."

"A nerd is into engineering and math. A geek is …" He gives another shrug. This one inexplicably even more awkward. "I don't know. Cooler, I guess."

I bust out laughing and have to put down the soup because I don't want to spill it on his fancy-ass (probably) cashmere throw. "Are you serious right now?"

He gives me a thoughtful look. "About what?"

I drop my voice and mimic his tone. "A geek is cooler."

His jaw clenches and—if possible—the red flushing his cheeks deepens. "I guess I don't need to ask if you're feeling better, since you obviously are."

He makes to stand, but I reach out and grab his arm before he can stalk away. "I'm sorry. Seriously. I will stop teasing you." He squints like he doesn't believe me, so I hold out my hands again in a sign of innocence. "But dude, you are about the coolest person I've met. So you'll have to excuse me if that whole I'm-not-as-cool-as-a-geek argument took me by surprise."

He slowly sits back down, frowning and still looking flustered. He looks like he wants to dig for more information, but doesn't want to outright ask, opening his mouth and then snapping it shut again.

I take pity on him. "You are obviously rich and insanely good looking." He makes a scoffing noise at that last bit. I pick up my soup and poke at it absent-mindedly so he won't notice how awkward I feel admitting I find him attractive. He isn't traditionally handsome, with his nose that is a little too big, but somehow balanced out by his soulful eyes and wide, full lips. And don't even get me started on his body. He's not like some jacked Instagram model, but he's unexpectedly fit and strong in a way that makes me feel safe. When I realize I'm staring at him, I swallow and add, "And unless I'm mistaken, ridiculously smart as well."

He clears his throat. "I don't know about—"

"Were you or were you not talking on the phone just now about how to solve climate change?"

I pin him with a look.

He blushes again. "Well, climate change isn't something any one person is going to solve."

"But that is what you're working on?"

"I'm just trying to figure out which scientists have the best shot at solving it and making sure they have the funding to do so."

"Again, because you're rich and smart." He shrugs, still looking embarrassed. "So, to recap: You're rich, smart, and working on saving the world. Basically, you're a superhero. It doesn't get any cooler than that."

He says nothing in response, just does that thing with his jaw, working the muscles like he wants to say something and doesn't have the words. Somehow—I don't know how I know, but I know— somehow, I know what he's thinking. He's thinking about that ex of his. Ava, the movie star. The woman who broke his heart and bad mouthed him all over late night. The woman he maybe bought this house for, before she broke up with him.

Somehow I know he's thinking that if he had been cooler, she wouldn't have left him.

Imagining those thoughts in his head ... it breaks my heart a little. And makes me want to stab her.

I don't think of myself as prone to violence, but I better never meet that bitch alone in a dark alley, because I have a butcher knife and an industrial food processor. I could make her disappear.

Instead of threatening violence to a woman he is clearly still in love with, I try to think of something I can say that might give him some comfort. Some scrap of peace.

I want to tell him she's not worth it. That if she

couldn't see how amazing he is, then she didn't deserve him. I want to grab him by the shoulders, give him a hard shake, and tell him to get the fuck over her. To tell him that there are other fish in the sea. Hell, there are other fish right here on his sofa.

Thank God, I come to my senses before I can say any of that garbage out loud.

Because Ian is a genuinely (if somewhat unexpectedly) good guy. For all the reasons I just listed and more.

And he doesn't need to know his personal chef is nursing a crush on him. Maybe more than a crush.

So, instead, I burrow a little deeper into the covers and say the only thing I can think of to make light of the situation. "See, now I just want to rewatch the Avengers."

He slants me a confused look. "What? Why?"

"Come on! You're basically Tony Stark. But without the Iron Man suit."

He blinks as if surprised by the comparison. Then chuckles and plays along. "No one has an Iron Man suit, because that technology doesn't exist."

"Whatever. I'm sure you could invent it if you weren't so focused on fixing climate change, you selfish bastard." I kick him again playfully. "Now cue up some Marvel for me."

I half expect him to start up a movie and leave

me to it, but instead, he settles in and watches with me. At some point, he makes popcorn and brings me more tea. I stretch out my legs and my feet end up in his lap. He doesn't complain when I insist we skip Civil War, because it's too depressing. I drift off during Infinity War and when I wake up, I'm back in his bed, tucked in with my cat asleep at my feet.

sixteen

IAN

The day Savannah showered—her third day at my house—I walked back up to her cottage while she was sleeping on the sofa and brought back a duffle bag of clothes and toiletries for her. On her fourth day at my house, she was strong enough to walk downstairs on her own. She said she felt fine, but I could tell she was lightheaded. I insisted she stay another day rather than try to make it all the way up the hill to her cottage. Besides, she'd fallen asleep early in Infinity War. Since neither of us had seen it or Endgame, she stayed to watch those.

On the fifth day, she might have felt well enough

to walk up to the cottage, but we hadn't watched The Guardians of the Galaxy movies yet.

On the sixth day, she felt well enough to cook, but by then I was behind on work. She was strong enough to move back to the cottage, but I was too busy to carry Mr. Sniggles and all his gear up the hill, and I certainly couldn't let her do it.

That cat is huge. Even if I could have helped her get him into the cat carrier, she wouldn't be able to carry him.

On the morning of the seventh day, Mr. Sniggles was hiding under the bed and refused to come out until it was nearly dinner time.

Savannah had had groceries delivered at noon, and that probably scared him. By the time he snuck out to see if we were all okay, she'd already started making dinner.

And, yes, by this point I'd admitted the truth to myself. I don't want her to leave.

Ever.

This past week, we'd slipped out of our boss/employee roles and into something different. Something unlike anything I'd ever had with a woman. Hell, unlike anything I'd ever had with anyone. I have no illusions that this symbiotic relationship we're developing means as much to her as it did to me, but that didn't seem to matter.

There was no one else I'd ever known that I felt comfortable just being with. But it was different with her.

Yes, I want her so badly it nearly hurts just being around her. But even this odd state of friend zone limbo is better than nothing. More importantly, she seems comfortable in the friend zone. Relaxed even as she snuggles up next to me on the sofa, our legs stretched out in front of us, sharing a huge bowl of popcorn.

She's paused the movie, going into a mini rant lecture about the soundtrack, when I take her left hand in mine and look at her palm.

"I've been wanting to ask." I trace the tattoo on her palm. It's two concentric circles, the smaller one about the size of a nickel, the larger about the size of a half dollar.

"About the tattoos?"

I nod.

She wiggles her right arm free from under the popcorn bowl and points to the smaller circle. "This is a teaspoon." Then she runs her finger over the larger circle. "And this is a tablespoon."

I look from her palm back up to her face, only to get momentarily lost in the brilliance of her gaze. "A teaspoon and a tablespoon?"

She shrugs. "Yeah. While I'm cooking. So I can pour seasoning into my palm to measure it."

I look at her palm again. "That can't be very accurate. Especially for liquids."

She tips her head back and laughs, practically a full-bodied guffaw. "It's not. Especially for liquids. But for things that aren't liquids—salt, sugar, flour, that kind of thing—it's close enough. All of cooking is an approximation. Seasoning is affected by all the other ingredients, anyway. No two steaks are identical. No two mushrooms or squash. You can't measure once and assume the food is well-seasoned. You have to taste it, adjust, and taste again. That's the only way to get it right."

I trace my finger over the lines in her palm. "Then why even bother with the measurements?"

"When I got them, I was young and less experienced. Precise measurements seemed to matter more back then. Plus, it seemed like all chefs have tattoos." Tipping her head to the side, she studies her palm. "I don't really use them anymore, but I still love them. They remind me that every meal is unique. Even things that look identical are special."

She is looking at her hand, but I'm soaking in all the details of her. The way some of her hair always slips out of the knot on top of her head, but she never seems to notice. The way the faint battle scars on her arms from her life as a chef remind me of Ogham, the ancient Pictish writing made up of slashed lines etched into stone. The way her imperfections make her only more beautiful.

She has never been more right. She is unique and special in a way that no other beautiful woman is.

When she shifts from looking at her hands to look at me, I jerk my gaze back to the iPad that's still resting on my lap beside the popcorn bowl.

"Oh, do you have work to do?" she asks, nodding in the direction of my iPad. "Do you want to read instead of watching the movie?"

"No. I like watching movies with you," I tell her, because I can't tell her what I really want to say. That anything I do with her is better than anything else I could be doing alone.

She slants a suspicious look in my direction. "Really? Because I call bullshit."

"What?"

"You say that, but I know it's not really true."

"I would never lie to you."

She rolls her eyes. "Okay, but the whole time I was sick, you would sit with me and watch TV, but you clearly turned it off whenever I fell asleep and you went right back to reading stuff for work."

"Yes, that's true." I nod. "But why would that make you think I don't like watching TV with you?"

"You're obviously humoring me. If you really like watching The Avengers or Brooklyn Nine-Nine or whatever, you would just keep watching it after I fell asleep instead of pausing and waiting for me to wake up again."

"There is a flaw in your logic."

"Really? Oh, please, wise Ian, explain the flaw in my logic," she says in a tone that I'm growing to recognize as her teasing me.

"You're assuming that when I claim to enjoy watching TV with you, that it's the show on TV that I enjoy."

She shakes her head, looking bemused and amused. "So you enjoy watching TV with me, but not watching TV?"

"Exactly. It is being with you that makes watching things interesting."

She sucks in a breath and studies me, before asking simply, "Why?"

Somehow, her hands are in my hands again. Her palm is turned up and I find myself tracing the concentric circles on her palm trying to put my feelings about her into words.

"I've never felt ... human. I've always felt like I'm something else. Some slightly different species of hominid." I glance at her, trying to judge how crazy this sounds to her.

She just nods. "A lot of people on the spectrum say they feel that way. Like they're alien visitors from another planet."

A rush of relief hits me, even though that is not a description I've heard before. "Exactly. There are some people who are easier to be with, like my mom and Martin. But you are the easiest to be with."

seventeen

SAVANNAH

My left hand is still in his and he's tracing the concentric circles when I automatically bring my right hand up to cup his jaw.

Despite how close we've become this week, I've never touched him. Not like this. Sure, the occasional brushing of my knuckles against his in the popcorn bowl. My legs stretched out next to his on the sofa. My feet burrowing under his leg when my toes get cold. But nothing like this. Nothing deliberate. Nothing intentional.

Nothing that speaks to my need to touch this particular man, in this moment. This man who is like no other man I've ever known. In the moment that I could share with no other person.

Because Ian is so uniquely himself. And because no other person has ever asked these kinds of thoughtful, probing questions or listened to my answers in quite the same way. No one else has ever shared so much of themselves, or trusted me with such delicate insights into who they are.

I want to tell him all of that, and I'm also afraid to, because I don't want to reveal how much he means to me. How far in I am already. If my feelings scare me this much, I can only assume they'll terrify him.

So I don't voice any of that out loud. Instead, I get lost in the sensation of his cheek under my palm. Because his hair is dark, he seems to have a perpetual scruff on his jaw. I've seen him almost clean shaven, only to have it popped back up within a few hours. On him, the scruff doesn't seem like an artful pretense. Its ever-changing length speaks more to negligence than intention.

Still, seeing that scruff day after day didn't prepare me for the sensation of it against my palm. For a moment, I simply get lost in the feel of it prickling against my skin. Until he speaks.

"Savannah..." My name comes out like a prayer. His raspy voice pitched lower than normal.

I pull my gaze from his cheeks up to his eyes, but I say nothing, because it feels like anything I say will only break the spell.

And I don't want to be the one to do that.

If the spell breaks, it's going to have to be by him.

He clears his throat. "Savannah, this isn't a good idea."

"Why not?" I know all the reasons it's a bad idea on my end and none of them are enough to keep me from wanting it, anyway.

"I'm your boss, for starters."

"You're not. Martin is my boss."

"There's still a power dynamic I'm not comfortable with."

"Because of the money?"

He just nods.

"Bad news, buddy. As far as I can tell, you're insanely rich. If you're going to limit yourself to sleeping with women who have as much money as you do, your dating pool just got miniscule."

His lips twitch. "That's not what I meant. Even if I'm not your boss, you still depend on me for money. Your salary comes from my estate. And I know—"

He cuts himself off, and I get the feeling he's on the verge of saying that he knows how desperately I need my salary. I don't like the way that makes me feel or the resentment it stirs up in me. Not at him. None of this is his fault. But I still resent being this poor when I thought I was doing everything right.

Moreover, I don't want to be thinking about my poverty or Blake or my fucked up finances right now.

It's a splash of bitters in an otherwise perfectly balanced drink.

Besides I'm tired of letting Blake have any say in my life. Of letting what he did control my fate.

"However badly you think I need the money, I need it less badly than I did six months ago. I could quit tomorrow and I would be so much better off than I was before I took this job. I could quit tonight if that's what you need."

His eyes flash at the phrase *what you need*. His gaze moves over my face, taking in every aspect of my expression, as if he's searching for answers.

"That's not what I meant," he murmurs.

It's not an answer. Not really. It's not a yes. It's not consent. But it's enough for me. I shift on the sofa, swinging one leg over him to straddle his hips, slowly lowering myself down, giving him plenty of time to say no. He doesn't.

His eyes flash again, but with something darker. He releases my hand to settle both of his palms on my hips. Pulling me forward just enough, so the apex of my thighs comes in contact with the long hard ridge of his cock.

"Savannah."

He says it like it's the beginning of a sentence, like there's more he wants to say, but doesn't. I give him space to say more. When he doesn't, I lower my mouth to his.

IAN

I like to think of myself as a logic man. A man of above average intelligence. A man who has at least a modicum of control over his actions.

Yeah. That's what I like to think.

But the moment Savannah's mouth touches mine, all that goes out the window.

Logic?

An illusion.

Intelligence?

Say what now?

Restraint?

Phfff...

Logic, intelligence, and control are for other

men. For some earlier, dumber version of myself, who couldn't even imagine a moment like this.

A me who didn't have the most beautiful, irresistible woman in the world straddling his lap, rubbing against his cock, cupping his face in her hands as she kisses him.

Her first kiss is slow. Hesitant. Almost a question in physical form.

After the briefest brush of her lips against mine, she pulls back, her gaze moving over my face like she's looking for answers to some question she hasn't voiced out loud.

For once, I seem to know what she's thinking.

Me, who never knows what anyone is thinking and barely believes them if they tell me in words. Somehow, I know what she's thinking. So I say it out loud for her.

"Are we really doing this?"

Her lips twitch into a half smile, her gaze alight with heat. And with something else. Something I've never seen in a woman's gaze when I've kissed her. Something I don't associate with sex at all.

I see humor. Delight. A kind of unrestrained joy that seems both out of place in this moment and like what's been missing from every other encounter I've ever had with a woman.

This moment—with her on my lap, the barest

taste of her on my lips—seems to stretch out to eternity, the energy zipping back and forth between us. I feel so connected to another person I can imagine what she's thinking as easily as I can envision an elegant coding solution.

And just like that, I can imagine an entire future with Savannah. One where she cooks for me and dances around my kitchen and sends me snarky texts when I don't pay enough attention to her. One where she makes me stop working long enough to watch movies and eat popcorn with her, and I don't resent the intrusion. One where she kisses me. Where I kiss her, whenever I want. One where kissing is joyous and spontaneous and not some serious production involving candles and lingerie and the pretense of desire.

She rolls her lip beneath her teeth as if biting down on her lip is the only way to keep herself from laughing.

God. She's so fucking beautiful I can hardly bear to look at her, but I certainly can't look away.

She nods. "Yeah. I guess we are."

It takes me a second to realize that she's answering the question I asked out loud a second ago. A lifetime ago, in my mind and in my imagination.

Are we really doing this? Yes, she guesses we are.

My breath catches in my throat and for a second I'm afraid to move, because there's no way I'm not going to fuck this up. There's no way I can actually be who she wants. That I can be clever enough, passionate enough, good enough in bed for her.

But fuck that shit ...

She's here. She's with me. Maybe we'll have that amazing future I just imagined. Maybe we won't. Maybe I'll fuck this up. Maybe I won't.

All I know is that I want this woman more than I've ever wanted anything in my life. I have no idea if I can be enough for her. But I know I have to try.

And I know I want to try. I want to be everything she wants. I want to be her everything.

She quirks her eyebrows like she's lobbing a silent question back at me. Do I want this, too?

Yeah. Abso-fucking-lutely.

"Okay, then," I say out loud.

With my palms still on her hips, I stand, picking her up with me. Thank God for leg day. She squeals as I sling her over my shoulder, fireman-style and head for the stairs.

nineteen

SAVANNAH

I knew Ian was strong, but I'm still surprised when he stands, lifting me with him as if I weigh absolutely nothing. He tosses me over his shoulder like I'm a rag doll and practically jogs up the two flights of stairs to his bedroom on the third floor.

I'd complain if the view of his ass wasn't so good. And if his speed didn't convey that he's just as eager as I am.

He tosses me on the center of his bed, then crawls up between my legs, skimming his hands along the outside of my pants.

His pants, actually.

He brought up a duffle bag of my clothes a

couple of days ago. I welcomed the panties and bras, but never quite transitioned from wearing his over-sized sweatpants and T-shirts back into wearing my own clothes. I kept waiting for him to say something about it. But he hasn't.

Until now.

Now, as soon as he reaches the waistband of the sweatpants, he bunches the hem of the shirt in his hands. I lift my hips so he can free the back of the shirt. He doesn't move to take the shirt all the way off but bares only my belly before settling between my legs to rain kisses on the skin he's exposed.

He's kissing his way down my stomach, inching the waistband of the sweatpants down as he goes, when I'm struck with a burst of panic as I realize what he'll find when he pulls my sweats all the way off. My sweats that are actually his sweats. And that I haven't been wearing any underwear under. Gah. Is that going to gross him out?

I plant my palms on his shoulders. "Wait. Stop."

My words come out sounding like more of a gasp than a request, but he stills instantly, looking up at me.

His gaze roves my face, as intense and serious as ever.

"What is it?" He moves to pull back with a decisive nod. "You don't want this."

"No, that's not it." My hands clench on his shoulders, trying to hold him in place, close to me, but also still so I have a moment to think. "Don't ... I just ..."

"What is it?" he asks again, a note of real concern in his voice.

He's lying between my legs, half up on one elbow as he studies me. We're both still fully clothed, but despite that it is possibly the most intimate position I've ever been in. Certainly the most intimate *conversation* I've ever had. For me, sex has always been a bit perfunctory. A thing to do and be done with. Pleasant. Good. Sometimes even great. But never something to discuss. To talk about.

But suddenly I feel this need to talk to Ian before we go any farther. At the very least to give him a heads up.

"Here's the thing. You know how I started wearing your sweatpants and T-shirts because I showered and didn't have any clothes here?"

He nods, eyes suddenly alight with mischief. "Yeah."

"And then I just sort of never stopped wearing your clothes. And you never said I should. Even though you brought me clothes from my cottage."

His lips twitch in a smirk. "Because seeing you in my clothes is so fucking hot, it makes me crazy."

"Glad you think that." I release a huff of breath, biting down on my lip. "Because I didn't have any clean underwear that first day. And so I didn't put any on under your sweatpants. I haven't been wearing underwear, even though you brought me clothes. Because I liked how your clothes felt against my skin."

Ian has gone completely, stone still. He's frozen in place. Not even breathing by the time I finish talking. He's just staring at me, his expression somewhere between shocked and …

I don't know what.

I can't tell what he's thinking. It's been pretty obvious that he has sensory issues of some kind. I'd have to be the most insensitive twat ever not to have noticed. And also, maybe he's on the spectrum or something. So … I don't know. Maybe this information has horrified him. Repelled him.

"Say something."

My words seem to snap him out of his spell, but not in a good way.

He rolls away from me, to sit on the edge of the bed, head buried in his hands.

Oh, fuck.

This is bad.

Horrible.

I have killed the moment and possibly freaked him out. Definitely ruined everything.

I scramble to my knees and move behind him. I reach out my hand to hover over his shoulder, but stop just shy of touching him.

"I'm so sorry. I didn't think it would be that big a deal. Or that you would even find out. I know it's weird or icky or whatever and—"

I cut myself off when he turns his head to look at me. His irises are blown wide, his gaze dark and stoney. His breath coming sharp through his parted lips.

"It's not," he says on a rasp.

"What?"

He stands, turning to face me, his gaze moving up and down my body where I'm kneeling on his bed, then settles on the juncture of my thighs.

"It's not weird. It's certainly not icky." He clears his throat, running his hand down his front to grip his cock through his own pair of gray sweatpants. "It's the hottest fucking thing I've ever heard." He gives his cock a squeeze and tug, like he can't not touch himself. "The idea that you've been walking around this house for days without underwear on." He shivers, his hand clenching. "While wearing only my clothes? It's ... I can't..."

His expression is stretched so tight he looks like

he might crack, but it's not his facial expression that holds my attention. It's the slow, steady movement of his hand, gripping his dick through his sweats, tugging up and down.

I was wet before, but now I'm drenched.

"Then why'd you stop?"

He tears his gaze up to my face. "It's too much. I want you too much."

Relief floods through me. Relief. Desire. Glee.

It's one jumbled flood of feelings and need and it bubbles out of me. "Impossible."

"I've never wanted anyone the way I want you. I don't want to lose control."

"Maybe that's exactly what I want you to do."

"I don't want to be too rough. I don't want to hurt you."

His hand stills.

I don't know the right thing to say here.

I know he would never hurt me. That he couldn't possibly hurt me.

Whatever he's feeling, however big and over-whelming it feels to him, it's not too much, because I'm right there with him.

He's not alone in this compulsive need. This urgency that I can't put into words and don't know how to explain.

The one thing I do know is that words won't be

enough. I can't tell him all the ways I want him. I can't explain why I'm not afraid of him being too rough or how I know that it's going to be perfect. Ian is a man who lives so much in his own head that he'll be able to talk himself around anything I try to put into words.

So I don't talk.

Or rather I don't only talk.

I crawl to the edge of the bed, gripping his hips in my hands before he can step back.

"Savannah." He says my name on a breath and a prayer.

I lower myself so I'm sitting on the edge of the bed, my legs on either side of his, my hands still gripping his hips, my face just the right height to press a kiss on his stomach through his T-shirt.

"Okay, let me see if I've got this straight. You're worried that you want me too much. That you'll lose control and hurt me." He moves like he's going to take a step back, so I wrap my legs around his, locking my ankles behind his legs, keeping him trapped. "Do I have that right?"

twenty

IAN

It takes me a minute to see where she's going with this.

Little wonder where there's exactly no blood flow to my brain right now.

How could there be blood anywhere other than my cock when Savannah is on my bed, her legs wrapped around me, looking up at me like that?

I can hardly be blamed for not catching where she's going with this until her hands slip under the waistband to shove my sweatpants and my boxers down my hips. She cups my ass as she lowers them past my ass and runs her hands around to free my cock.

"Savannah, you don't—"

But she doesn't give me a chance to finish the thought. She runs her tongue up the length of my cock to circle the head.

"If you're worried you'll lose control and hurt me if we have sex, then you just need to lose control before we start."

She wraps her lips around the head, her cheeks hollowing as she gives my cock one long suck.

And that's all it takes.

Just my dick in her mouth.

Except it's not just that. It's everything about this moment. It's everything that has led up to this moment. It's her living in my house. Her sleeping in my bed. Her wearing my clothes. It's the thought of her pussy naked beneath those clothes for the past week.

Fuck, no wonder I feel like I'm constantly surrounded by the scent of her. Her pussy has been right there all along. So close.

And that's why I lose it.

I grip the back of her head and pump into her mouth just once before I come. She doesn't have a chance to swallow, because I come so hard and so fast. It's exactly what I was afraid of.

A fucking mess.

I make a mess of her.

I come in her mouth and on her lips and her chin.

By the time I'm done, she's filthy, gloriously covered in my come.

I've never seen anything more gorgeous than my come painting her face.

Except for her smile, that is. Except for the way she grins up at me.

I run one hand down the back of her head, tipping her chin up with the other as I groan. "That was fucking embarrassing."

I try to wipe the come off her chin with my thumb, but her lips chase it and she sucks my thumb into her mouth, licking it clean with relish.

"That was fucking hot, is what that was," she says, releasing my thumb with a pop and then nipping at my hand like she can't get enough of me.

This woman, this gorgeous, amazing, brilliant woman wants me. Can't get enough of me. Just let me come all over her.

What the hell did I ever do to deserve her? To deserve this?

Before I can question it, I pick her up and throw her to the center of the bed. I follow her, pulling those sweatpants down her legs to reveal, just as she promised, her naked pussy.

I spread her legs wide with my shoulders and

just look, taking in her soft folds, glistening with her desire. Her curls are trimmed but not waxed bare. Until this moment, I didn't know I had a preference, but the second I see Savannah's tight cropped curls, I know this is it. It's perfect. She's perfect.

I lean in close, inhaling the heady scent of her, before running my tongue up her seam. She arches against my mouth when I press the flat of my tongue on her clit. I feel her flutter against my lips as I suck her clit into my mouth, wishing I could devour her.

The taste of her, the sounds she makes, the scent of her, it's all overwhelming. It's everything I need and not enough all at the same time. I slide a finger inside of her, finding her g-spot, stroking it in rhythm to the motion of my mouth. By the time she comes in a series of full body shudders, I'm hard again. Maybe, impossibly, even harder than before.

But that's how she makes me feel. Like every moment with her is more impossibly perfect than the last.

Her body is still trembling when I pull myself up, pushing myself to my knees between her legs. I pull her body up with me, her legs hooked on either arm, my hands anchoring her hips, my cock lined up perfectly to her cunt. I slid in while the last of her climax is still trembling through her walls. My dick finds that perfect spot where my fingers just were. My thumbs, her clit. My hips, the rhythm we both need.

I pound into her, driving us both to another climax, to the point of collapse. And when it's done, when I've come inside her, I lower her down and collapse on top of her, my dick still inside her. I bury my face in her neck, hiding whatever this is that she's pulled out of me.

Not just a climax, but something more. A groan. A sob. I don't know what.

I may have made a mess of her, but she's fucking wrecked me.

# twenty-one

SAVANNAH

I would've thought it would be weird, cooking for Ian after spending the night having sex with him. As if it's blurring a boundary that I should want to keep in place.

But it doesn't feel weird. And it doesn't feel like there's a boundary there at all. Not anymore. After last night, there are no boundaries. No barriers.

In every sense of the word. Before Ian, I've never had unprotected sex. Not that it was really unprotected, because I'm on birth control. And we discussed our mutual clean health afterwards. Still, not discussing it first isn't something I've ever done before. Part of me feels like I should be at least a little freaked out by how much I instinctively trust Ian, but on the other hand, look what he's like with me.

No one has ever taken such good care of me. I don't know that there's anyone else I would *let* take care of me like this. Maybe that too should scare me, but I don't want to be scared. I don't want to worry about the future. I just want to wallow in this delicious, comfortable intimacy.

So, when I wake up before him for the first time since I got sick, I get up to make him breakfast. Oddly enough, he sleeps through me climbing out of bed, sneaking off to the bathroom to clean myself up a bit, and then heading downstairs to the kitchen.

Probably because he got so little sleep when I was sick. All of those days of me drifting in and out of sleep in his bedroom and always having him there by my side in the few minutes I was awake. Besides, I know there's only one bed in this house and until last night he hadn't slept in it in over a week. Sleeping in chairs or on the sofa for the week can't have been easy for a man as tall as he is.

Since he seems inclined to sleep in, I let him. I sneak downstairs and start coffee. I dig around in the fridge to assess the food situation. Yesterday I wanted to make dinner, but he refused to let me anywhere near the kitchen, ordering take out again.

The fridge isn't as empty as I feared, but we're out of a lot of stuff. I find my phone—which I had abandoned in the living room the night before—and cue up my bossa nova Spotify list as I put in a grocery order to be picked up later today. Then I start biscuits, which I figure are the perfect food for today, since I'm not sure when he'll get up. They'll be best fresh out of the oven, but that's still twenty minutes away. And they'll still be good at any point during the day.

Once the biscuits are in the oven, I dig in the deep freeze and find some of the mixed berries I've been making smoothies with. I get them started on the stove top making a compote to go on the biscuits.

The biscuits are baking away in the oven and the house is starting to smell amazing as I dance around the kitchen, cleaning up the dishes from the biscuits, when I hear Ian clear his throat from behind me.

I whirl around hand pressed to my chest. "You startled me."

He's standing in the doorway to the kitchen, his shoulder propped on the door jamb, arms crossed over his chest as he watches me.

"Obviously." There's something needy and possessive in his eyes, but something a little sad as well. Something I can't quite read. He clears his throat again. "Sorry. I didn't mean to sneak up on you."

"It's okay. Was the music too loud?" I ask moving to the coffeemaker to pour him a cup. I walk it over to him, setting it on the counter near where he stands. There's a hesitancy in his posture that I don't like. And I can almost hear him second guessing himself. Second guessing us.

That won't do it all.

When it comes to business, science, and math, he is confident to the point of arrogance. When it comes to this kind of thing—interactions with another person—it's something else entirely.

I don't give him a chance to think too long about what happened last night, but walk right up to him and put my arms around his neck, pulling his head down to mine to kiss him. There's that same moment of resistance I sensed last night, before his hands drop to my hips and he pulls me to him, deepening the kiss on his own. I can feel the length of him hard against my belly.

He backs me up a step until my hips bump into the counter behind me. I want to let him keep going, but the biscuits are nearly done. So I pull back just enough to meet his gaze and grin. "Good morning."

He gives me a smoldering look and then drops

his head to my neck and nuzzles the spot behind my ear. "Good morning. You were up early."

"What can I say? I slept well last night."

Before I can say anything more, the timer on the oven goes off. I pull away and dance over to the oven to check on the biscuits. When I pull them out, all golden brown deliciousness, he says, "You were up really early."

"I hope you like biscuits."

"Is there anyone who doesn't?"

"Stupid people."

He reaches for a biscuit, and I swat his hand away. "You need to let them cool at least five minutes. Trust me, you don't want to burn the roof of your mouth."

He retrieves his coffee and takes a sip, then asks, "Who taught you how to dance?" A quirked eyebrow, and he nods toward the speaker where the bossa nova is playing.

My cheeks flush a little as I imagine him watching me as I danced around the kitchen doing the dishes. But out loud, I ask, "Who taught you how to not dance?"

He frowns, trying to parse my sentence. The confusion that flickers over his expression makes me chuckle. "It's just something my mom used to say. She and my dad always danced in the kitchen while they were making dinner. It was her favorite thing in the world." Sadness washes over me for a second, but I push it aside. "That was something she used to say. Nobody learns to dance. We're born knowing how to do it. We're taught how to not dance."

On impulse, I cross to where he's standing and stop several inches away, holding my left hand to hover at his shoulder, my other out beside my waist as if I'm poised to dance with him.

He arches his brow in silent question.

"Come on," I urge. "Let me show you."

Since we're right next to the biscuits, I snag a corner to taste-test while I wait for him.

"Hey!" He sounds indignant. "Why do you get to try the biscuits and I don't?"

"Trained professional." I point to myself. "Now, come on. Trust me."

I gesture him closer. This time, he steps forward with a droll look.

One hand settles on my hip as he takes my other in his. He keeps a respectful several inches between us, damn him. Yes, I was kind of hoping he'd close the distance between us, taking the opportunity to grind against me. But he doesn't. We could be on the set of Bridgerton.

"Okay," I coax. "Just listen to the rhythm and let your feet tell you what to do. I'll follow."

Before I can finish my thought, he starts dancing.

"Oh!"

He can dance!

It's not the sensual samba of a bossa nova, but classic Texas two step, the pace picked up to match the rhythm of the song.

He's a little rusty, but he moves with the confidence of a seasoned dancer. It's perfect.

He's perfect.

"You can dance." It comes out sounding like an accusation.

"Trained professional." He volleys my words back at me with a smirk.

I guffaw. "You are not a trained professional!"

"You don't know."

"Please tell me you didn't do one of those horrible dancing with the stars things when you first retired."

He laughs, a deep, genuine laugh. It's the first time I've ever heard him laugh, and it's a low, rich rumble that I feel all the way down to my cunt.

Oh, my. His laughter transforms him. It softens the hard edges of his face and takes him from interesting looking to devastatingly handsome.

Like the greedy addict I am, I can't get enough of

it. I want to make him laugh more. All day. Every day.

Because I feel like he probably hasn't laughed enough in his life and because I love that I'm the one who caused this miracle. Since I can't think of anything to keep him laughing, I go for keeping him dancing instead.

"Hey, Siri," I say. "Play something we can two-step to."

A moment later, a soft country music ballad starts, and he slows his steps to match, pulling me just a bit closer.

"Okay," I murmur. "Spill the beans. How'd you learn to dance like this?"

"Not Dancing with the Stars," he says.

"Thank God."

"My mom ..." He clears his throat, looking suddenly self-conscious. "She used to worry about me. Worried I didn't know how to interact with people. She enrolled me in one of those cotillion things when I was in high school."

"It paid off."

"It was horrible. Pure torture."

"Well, you're an excellent dancer now."

"It was the worst. If you think I'm awkward now, you should have seen me then. It was ten times worse."

My steps slow automatically as I gaze into his eyes. "I don't think you're awkward now."

I think you're perfect, I want to say.

Instead, I clear my throat and pick up my pace so we're back in rhythm with the song. "You've mentioned your mother several times, but never your father. What was his deal?"

I know as soon as I ask that it's a sensitive subject. I can feel it in the way his shoulders tense under my hand. "Never mind. You don't have to answer that. That was rude of me."

He clears his throat. "No. It's okay. Nothing you couldn't read online if you wanted. My father left us when I was just a kid. Five or six, I think."

"You think?" I ask. In for a nosy penny, in for a nosy pound. "You don't remember?"

"I don't have a lot of memories of him. Even before he left. I'm pretty sure Wikipedia has more information on him than I do." He gives a laugh that sounds more detached than bitter. "I read once that every great man has daddy issues." He snorts. "Not that I think I'm great. But I was young when I read that. It was motivation."

"And you haven't ever tried to find him?"

"Unnecessary. When you make as much money as I have, the unwanted relatives find you."

I want to hug him. Comfort him. Instead, I reach

my hand up to brush at a lock of his hair. "I'm sorry."

And I don't know if I'm apologizing for asking or offering consolation for what a douchebag his father is.

He stares off into the middle distance for a moment before bringing his gaze back to mine. "What about you? You've mentioned both your parents. Did your mom teach you to dance and cook?"

"Oh, no, the cooking was all Dad."

Confusion flickers over his face, and I realize we've never talked about my dad.

"My dad was Richard Lewis."

Ian's expression is blank, and he seems to be waiting for me to continue, so I add on a few descriptors. "Owner of Embarcado. He won Top Chef Masters, as well as a bunch of other awards."

"Ah. So he was one of those celebrity chefs?"

"He hated that phrase. He always said that the food is the star, not the person cooking it."

"So he taught you to cook."

My steps slow again, the memories of my father dragging my spirits down. "Taught sounds intentional. It wasn't. I was just ... always a daddy's girl. I wanted to be with him every moment he was home. He traveled a lot–for all of those being-not-a-celebrity-chef events. So whenever he was home, I wanted to be with him. That meant being in the kitchen of his restaurant. All the time. When you're around a kitchen that much, when food is the center of everything you do, you just absorb it. He never taught me to cook, but every conversation we ever had was about food."

Somehow we're still dancing, and Ian pulls me closer, wrapping his arms around me in something that's almost a hug as we sway back and forth.

I rest my head on his chest. It's all the physical closeness I've been craving, but it's not sexy or sensual. It's just … comfortable. And comforting.

With my head resting against his chest, I can say things out loud that I've never admitted to anyone.

"It doesn't sound healthy when I say it out loud. And I guess I knew that already, because now I think of all the things we never talked about. Not just the emotional stuff, like whether or not he loved me, but the big stuff, too. The practical things. Like who he wanted to run the restaurant after he died." I laugh, a bitter, unkind sound that makes me realize we've both stopped dancing. "I guess you're not that only with daddy issues."

"What happened to the restaurant?" There's a hesitancy in his voice, like he knows the answer, but also knows I won't talk about it unless he pushes.

"My dad died unexpectedly. He hadn't changed his will since he divorced his first wife. My mom got the house and the money in the bank, but everything else went to Blake."

"Blake?"

"My half-brother. He worked at the restaurant with us. He ran the front of the house and I ran the back of the house."

"It seems like you should've gotten an equal share of the restaurant."

"Seems like it, doesn't it? The funny thing is, Blake was never really interested in the restaurant until I started running the back of the house when I was twenty-two. Then he was all over it. Demanded he get a job there, too. And I'm not going to say he didn't work hard, because he did. I thought we got along. Thought we made a good team."

"You started running the back of the house at twenty-two? Isn't that a little young to be running a kitchen?"

I shrug. Trying to make light of it, even though I know how it looked. I didn't then, but I've had a lot of time to think about it since then.

"I guess. Probably people thought my dad gave me too much responsibility. Maybe they resented it." That's certainly how they made it sound when things came out in depositions. That I was incompetent. That I hadn't known how to do my job. Even though the restaurant flourished when Blake and I were working as a team. We made more money, sold more food, won more accolades together than dad ever had on his own. But I guess just enough of the staff resented me to make it seem like it was all Blake's doing. "I'd been working in the kitchen of that restaurant since I was fourteen. I knew it front and back. I could've done any job in the restaurant. So when dad decided to step back from the day to day stuff, it seemed natural that I take over as head chef."

"Fourteen? Is that a violation of child labor laws?"

"Not in Texas. In a family restaurant, you can officially start working there at fourteen."

"Does that mean you unofficially worked there younger?"

"No comment."

"So when your dad died, you'd been working there for over a decade. But your brother got the entire restaurant?"

"Pretty much. I tried to fight him at first." I laugh, a hard, bitter laugh that I don't like. "I thought it was just a misunderstanding. Something we could settle in mediation. I was wrong. The irony is that he didn't even want the restaurant. As soon as I ran out of money and dropped the lawsuit, he sold it. Now there's an Embarcado in every major tourist town in America."

Ian mutters a series of curses under his breath that I don't bother trying to distinguish. There's nothing he could say that would match the things I've said about Blake. About our justice system.

I'm long past blaming Blake. I'll never forgive him, but I don't know that I can forgive myself either.

"I was hopelessly naïve, assuming that family meant anything to him. But we grew up together, for fuck's sake. His own mom was ... temperamental. He spent more time with us than he did with her. And it was all just so ..." I let my words trail off, trying to put my thoughts together. "So messy. One minute, everything's fine. I'm going to work, doing the job. I wasn't thriving financially, but I did okay. The next, I got the call that my dad was in the hospital. My world crashed down around me. My dad was gone. People I'd worked with for a decade—People I thought respected me—turned their backs on me the moment they realized I didn't get the restaurant. Suddenly I was out of a job and practically unemployable."

"But you're a great chef."

I shrug. "My experience didn't really count for

much because everyone assumed I'd been coasting on my father's coattails."

"But you can obviously cook. I've eaten more good food in the past six months than I have in the rest of my entire life."

He sounds so indignant on my behalf. I nearly laugh, despite the somber mood. "Sure, I can cook. But I never went to culinary school. I never went to college. All of my education was hands-on. I'd only ever worked at Embarcado. And there was Blake, bad-mouthing me all over town. It makes it really fucking hard to find work. To make matters worse, I'd racked up all this legal debt. Pretty soon it looked like there was no way out. Then this lawyer calls me up, with this crazy offer to be a personal chef."

"Then you ended up here."

"And I ended up here."

He's frowning, like he's puzzling through something, and then he asks. "What will you do when the contract is up?"

"I have no idea. When I first took the job, all I could think of was getting out of debt."

"And now?"

I pull back to tip my head to the side and study him.

Now?

Now, I don't want to think about the contract

ending at all. If I think about what I'm going to do after my contract ends, then I have to remember that this *is* a contract. That Ian isn't my friend ... or whatever this is.

That he's not just some neighbor who took care of me while I was sick. We're not friends who live together and then had sex one night.

I put my head back on his chest, wishing he hadn't asked what I was going to do next. Wishing I could wind back time and skirt around this entire conversation about my dad and my failed career.

twenty-two

IAN

If you'd asked me when I woke up this morning if I could ever hold Savannah in my arms and not want to fuck her, I would have laughed in your face.

Which goes to show what a dumbass I am.

Clearly, it's not that I don't want her. I'm pretty sure I will always want her, every moment of every day for the rest of my life. But everything about this conversation is a boner-killer. So even though her body is pressed against mine, even though we're still swaying to the country music playing through the speaker in the kitchen, the urges I'm feeling are decidedly not sexual.

I don't want to fuck her. I want to keep holding

her. I want to soothe her. To stroke her hair. To take care of her.

Not unlike when she was sick, I just want her to feel better. And I want to be the one who does that for her. It's strange, this sudden need to alleviate someone else's discomfort. It's so foreign, it's almost intolerable.

And yet, I don't want it to end. In fact, when she tries to pull away, I almost don't let her go.

My arms tighten instinctively, but I release her, even though it feels like she's taking a chunk of me with her.

She turns, pacing to the far side of the kitchen. She faces the windows, looking at the view of the lake beyond.

"I'm sorry." Even though she's facing away from me when she moves her hands up to her face, I can tell she's brushing away tears.

"Why are you apologizing?"

"For making it weird. By talking about this at all. For crying in front of you." She makes a strangled sound that sounds half like a chuckle and half like a sob. "God, I hate crying in front of other people. Probably almost as much as other people hate when someone cries in front of them."

"Do other people hate that?"

She twists just enough to talk over her shoulder at me, one eyebrow raised. "Do you not hate that?"

"I don't know that anyone has cried in front of me before."

Or maybe they have, and I just haven't noticed.

Yeah, that sounds more likely.

I take a step closer to her, wishing that I could go all the way over to her and pull her back into my arms. "I don't mind that you're crying."

The opposite almost. It feels like a gift. Like something she wouldn't do in front of just anyone. Like it's a sign that she trusts me enough to be vulnerable in front of me. That doesn't feel like a nuisance. It feels like an honor.

Suddenly, I wish more people had cried in front of me. Maybe, then I would know what the right thing to say was. Maybe then I would know how to handle this. How to console her.

"I'm sorry you're sad."

My words feel inadequate, and I know it's the wrong thing to say because something like disgust flickers across her face.

"I'm not sad."

"Then what?"

"I'm mad." Before I can agree that she should be mad at her father and brother, she adds, "Mostly at myself, for being so stupid."

"You're not stupid." I think of all the times we talked about one of the grant proposals I was reading. "You've been able to discuss nearly every grant proposal I've ever discussed with you. You're obviously highly intelligent."

"I guess a lot of highly intelligent people are also dumbasses then."

"You're not—"

"I should've asked my dad. I should've talked to him about what his intentions were. If I'd known he would never leave me the restaurant, I would've gotten a different job. I would've had him write me a recommendation while he was still alive and gone to work at another restaurant. I shouldn't have assumed Blake would do the right thing when I filed the probate case. Looking back, I was so gullible. So naïve. So stupid."

"You said you were fourteen when you started working for your father."

She glances at me, meeting my gaze. "About."

"You were still a child. It's not naïve for a child to trust their parent. It's human nature."

"But—"

"There is no but. Children love their parents and trust their parents. Even children who are adults trust their parents. And most parents are trustworthy. The emotional strength of the bond between child and parents is the cornerstone of human soci-ety. That's how our species has survived. We are programmed to take care of one another. It's genetics and biology. It's woven into our DNA and our biochemistry. The people who betray loved ones are either sociopaths or narcissists. The people who are betrayed are not gullible. They're victims."

Surprise flickers over her features and some-thing else as well. Hurt, maybe.

Fuck. I've probably gone too far. It wouldn't be the first time I've handled a delicate situation badly.

"Wow, that sounds very ..." She blows out a breath and then releases a chuckle. "Psychologically accurate."

Not sure how to respond to that, I go with a safe, "Thank you."

Which was the wrong answer based on the way her chuckle morphs into a nervous laugh.

"Let me guess, one of those grant proposals you're always reading analyzed parent/child bonding?"

"No. That's just what my therapist used to say."

She blinks, then asks, "You've been to therapy?"

The way she says it ... not like it's something to be ashamed of or anything, but just the absolute shock in her voice. I can feel my cheeks heating up as I explain. "After Ava left. Yeah. She was the woman everyone thought I would marry. So when she left …"

I let my words trail off, unsure what to say and suddenly feeling very exposed.

When Ava left me, it shook me. Enough that I upended my life and went to months of therapy. One of the first things I realized in therapy was that my reaction wasn't about her at all. It was about how unhappy I was with my own choices. Which seems so obvious now. Now that I have Savannah in my life, I see so clearly how little Ava meant to me.

I'm not ashamed that I went to therapy. Clearly, I needed it. But in retrospect, I'm a little embarrassed that it was Ava leaving that caused me to go. Honestly, if I had gone to therapy before I met Ava, I never would've dated her.

I have to bite back the urge to say this to Savannah now. It can't be the right time to say that to her, can it? When we've only been together one night. And she still (indirectly) works for me. And we're in the middle of a messy conversation about her dad's betrayal.

So I keep my mouth shut. After a moment, she gives a tight nod. Expression still unreadable, she looks around the kitchen as if surprised to find herself there.

"I think I'm going to go home."

"What?"

"Just back to the cottage."

"Oh. Okay." I don't want her to leave, but it's not like I can keep her here. Kidnapping still being illegal and all.

She gives me a smile that seems a little forced, even to me, who normally doesn't notice that sort of thing and is always forcing myself. "It's been a long and weird week."

"How so?" I ask, before I can stop myself.

"Just ... the whole being sick thing. And you bringing me down here. Which I appreciate. Really." She gives an exaggerated double thumbs up. "You went above and beyond. Top-notch service. Five out of five stars. Would definitely recommend. But I think I should go back ... to my ... space. At the cottage. By myself for a bit."

She makes it almost to the door before she turns back and gestures to the biscuits sitting out on the counter.

"They should be ready to eat now. And don't forget the compote."

I watch her leave, more confused than ever.

Clearly, I did or said something wrong.

Maybe she just needs a little space. Or maybe I fucked everything up.

twenty-three

SAVANNAH

By the time I make it back to my cottage, I've realized three things:

1. I'm a coward for running away

2. This virus kicked my ass, because I'm out of breath before I even make it back to the cottage

3. I'll have to return to the main house, because I abandoned Mr. Sniggles there, like the worst cat mom ever

4. My phone has been here at the cottage all this time and I never even thought to ask about it

And, yes, I realize that's four things.

I'm just going to stop counting at four. The way

my life is going right now, if I keep on like this the list could get quite long.

A braver woman than I would grab my phone and immediately head back to the main house to rescue her cat. But I don't know that I have the emotional strength to face more heart-felt confessions from Ian and confront the sad state of my health all in one day. Especially not since Mr. Sniggles seems perfectly content to lounge around on Ian's expensive leather sectional.

Obviously, I will go steal my cat back at some point. Just not yet. Besides, I don't think I could take it if I march down the hill for my cat, only to have Mr. Sniggles give me the slightest sign that he'd rather stay with Ian.

Let's face it. Given the way today has been going, that seems likely.

Instead of thinking about Ian or Mr. Sniggles, I check my messages. I have a couple of voice mails from my mom, some text messages from people I used to work with, one from Dan asking if I still have his fillet knife (Um, no. I never did.), and a whole series of texts from Trinity.

> Hey, check in when you get a chance

How are you doing?

Helllooooooo????

For real

Answer me, damn it.

Okay, I'm seriously worried. The last I heard from you, you were sick. It's been six days. Are you dead? Are you in a pit somewhere putting lotion on your skin?

Would that even work? I feel like skin hydration at time-of-death can't be that important. I have a really lovely Coach tote and I can't believe they rubbed lotion on that cow for weeks before killing it.

OMG

What is wrong with you?

Also, I'm fine.

But seriously

Wtf?

I was worried.

You know I spiral when I'm worried. I get weird

Besides, you cook cows all the time. How is it okay to cook them but not discuss what happens to their skin after they die?

I don't know how to answer that.

But seriously

You're okay?

You went radio silent for six days!

I was about to contact the FBI

I don't think the FBI does that sort of thing

Okay, then Homeland Security

Or the police

Whatever

You were sick?

Yeah. Just a nasty cold

I'm fine now

Still confused

How did a cold keep you from texting back? Was it like a mutant virus that put you in a coma?

No. Just a normal cold

Then why u no text?

I was sick and Ian brought me down to his house so that he could take care of me. He forgot to bring my phone.

And ...????

And what?

You were away from your phone for six days!!!!

Either you were in a coma or something and-ish was going on.

And-ish?

You know ... something worthy of an *and*

And nothing.

OMG

You slept with him, didn't you?

Fess up

Fessupfessupfessupfessup!

I can see you working on your response and not sending it, so you obviously did.

I'm still waiting ....

Okay, if you don't want to admit that you slept with your boss, we don't have to talk about it. Just tell me, was it amazing?

Can we just not?

Does that mean it wasn't amazing or that it was so amazing you've lost the capacity to speak?

Please let it be the latter.

Can we be serious for a minute? I need to ask you a question.

So, you're just never going to tell me if it was amazing?

Was Dad a narcissist?

Whoa. That's a deep cut.

Where's this coming from?

Ian and I were talking about dad's death and how Blake got the restaurant.

And I admitted I felt stupid for not seeing it coming.

Lol.

Wait.

You're not serious, are you?

Yes.

Don't you feel stupid?

At least a little?

No.

Is that really how you feel?

Like what happened with Blake and the restaurant is your fault?

Yeah.

I guess it is really how I feel.

That is bullshit.

Dad didn't update his will

That's on him. He's the asshole here. And Blake. Blake's definitely an asshole

But, to answer your earlier question. Do I think dad was a narcissist?

A little. Maybe? Probably

My Ethics of Psychology prof says we should avoid diagnosing our relatives

Personally, I prefer the description, a bag of dicks

Trinity!

OK, real talk?

I know you always looked up to him. You were Daddy's perfect little girl.

You two had some sort of special bond, or whatever

But he wasn't a good father. He wasn't a good husband. He definitely wasn't a good boss. And honestly, I don't even think he was that good of a chef.

!!!!!

Oh, stop clutching your pearls.

I said what I said

He wasn't a bad chef, but he wasn't spectacular either. Frankly, I've always thought you could cook circles around him

Mostly, dad was charismatic. He was great in front of the camera. And he made a lot of people a lot of money. And that meant they spent a lot of time telling him he was amazing. I don't know whether or not that made him a narcissist.

But I do know this: you aren't stupid.

Wow

Did I stun you into silence?

Maybe. You definitely gave me a lot to think about.

Also …

Yeah?

I'm sorry.

For what?

You obviously had a lot of that locked and loaded. Which means you've thought about it a lot.

Yeah

Psych major, reporting for duty.

Your point?

I guess I didn't quite realize how different our childhoods were.

Btw, you don't have to apologize for any of this. Dad being a bag of dicks isn't on you. That's on Dad.

My therapist says that two people can grow up in the same house, but not in the same home.

I didn't know you'd been seeing a therapist.

A) again, psych major, so ... duh

B) doesn't everyone see a
therapist?

Apparently.

Wait. You don't?

I'm still trying to decide how to answer Trinity when my phone rings. I jump, because almost no one calls me. Sure, I get the occasional phone call from my mother, but beyond that, nothing. The last time I got regular phone calls was when we were in the height of the trial. Then, the phone calls always came from my lawyer. I now have a Pavlovian response of anxiety and nausea when my phone rings.

According to caller ID it's Martin. So I answer it.

"Savannah? It's Martin."

"Yes?"

"Where are you?" As always, Martin speaks in terse, short sentences. Like he's too busy for real conversation.

"Um ..." I'm not sure what the right answer is here.

"Are you at Ian's out by the lake?"

"Yes."

"Are you at the cottage or the main house?"

"The cottage. Why? Look, I know you're my boss, technically, but this line of questioning feels a little invasive."

"Sorry. I just—" He makes a noise of strangled frustration and for the first time I get the sense that he doesn't know what to say.

It's not like I've spent that much time with the guy, but every interaction we've had has been short and to the point. Succinct to the point of rudeness.

This sudden, apparent verbal awkwardness makes me nervous. "What's up?"

"I need you to trust me. And I need you to not repeat what I'm about to tell you. Not to anyone. Not even Ian, if he asks, though he probably won't. Can you do that?"

"No." I say succinctly. "If you're about to tell me that you're a serial killer, or that you've just assassinated Vladimir Putin, and you need me to help you bury the body, I can't promise I won't tell anyone."

"Jesus. Why are murder and dead bodies the first place you went with that? What is wrong with you?"

"Well, I just got off the phone with my sister and she has a way of making my imagination spin out."

He snorts. "Yeah. I can imagine."

He says it like he knows her and knows just how

annoying she can be. Under other circumstances, I might try to figure out what the deal is between the two of them, but this doesn't seem like the moment for that.

"Okay, as long as it's not illegal or immoral," I say. "You might as well tell me."

"I gather from Ian that he told you about his ex, Ava."

"I didn't violate the contract. He told me about her. I never even googled her. Or him, for that matter."

"Don't worry about that. The important thing is, you know they dated. You know she's bad news. Right?"

I think of how tied into knots Ian looks every time her name comes up. The way his voice catches when he says her name, as if he doesn't want to talk about her, but also can't not talk about her. "I think that's an understatement."

"I've reason to believe she's going to try to get Ian back."

"How could you know that?"

"Didn't you just say you didn't wanna know if it was illegal?"

"Okay. Continue."

"She's back in Austin. She got in this morning. And I don't know who she bribed or blew to find out, but she knows where Ian lives now and she's on her way out to see him."

"Oh."

"I don't trust her. And I don't trust him to be alone with her. She has a way of ... getting into his head."

"I don't know what you want me to do about it?"

"You're there. Can you just go down to his house and hang out. So that someone else will be with him when she shows up?"

"I don't think that's—"

"I was in Dallas for the weekend. I'm on the way now but I'm at least an hour away."

"He's a grown man. He doesn't need a chaperone."

"You don't know what she's like."

No. I don't know what she's like. But I know he loved her. Loves her?

God. I am so in over my head on this.

"You don't know what you're asking me to do. He's an adult. If he wants to see her, I don't know how I can keep him from doing that."

"I'm not asking you to physically bar the door from her. I just think that if there's a third person there it might... I don't know, keep her from getting in her claws into him."

"She's not a vampire."

"Close enough. She's a greedy manipulative bitch. She wants him for his money and his influence, nothing else."

"But if he loves her—"

"He doesn't. Trust me."

"So, what do you want me to do? Just go down and hang out in his house until she shows up?"

"Just go and be there. I don't care what excuse you give. As long as he doesn't have to be alone with her. I'll be there soon. Just stay there until I get there."

"And what are you gonna do once you show up? Or is this treading onto the territory of burying Vladimir Putin's body?"

"Let's hope it doesn't come to that. Will you do it?"

Do I want to do this? No. Absolutely not.

This is the last thing I wanna do today.

Martin says that Ian doesn't love Ava. But I'm pretty sure he does. Or at least he did. Am I really prepared to stand by while the man I'm falling in love with reunites with his ex?

No. No, I do not.

I can think of about five thousand things I would rather do, including rubbing lotion on my body in a pit.

But, if Martin is right, and Ava only wants Ian

back for his money and his influence, am I really prepared to let her just have him?

Even if he doesn't care about me, even if he only sees me as a friend and nothing more, shouldn't I try to protect him from her?

That's what a friend would do, right?

"Okay. I'll go down to the house. I'll be there and stay there until you show up."

"Thank you. And I'll make sure there's a bonus —"

"I swear to God, Martin, if you offer to pay me for this, I will buy the biggest zucchini I can find and shove it up your ass. And I won't even go to the trouble to make sure it's organic. It'll be conventionally grown, with all kinds of pesticides on it."

"Well, that's a hell of an image."

"I'm not doing this for you. And I'm not doing it for the money. I'm doing it because I care about Ian."

"Yeah. Okay." There's a bit of silence, and a note of something in his voice that I'm afraid might be awareness.

Fuck. Did I just admit to Ian's best friend that I'm in love with him?

"He's my friend too, and I don't wanna see him hurt by her anymore than you do." Hopefully, I emphasized friend enough to convince him.

"Shit!" I interrupt as a gleaming white SUV glides past the window heading towards the main house

"Stop being so dramatic. I'm not asking you to do anything illegal."

"No. She just arrived. I'll call you back."

I could debate it with myself as long as Ava showing up was hypothetical, but the second I see that SUV—the second I know Ava is here on his property about to go talk to Ian—I know the truth. I don't care whether he still loves her.

Or rather, thinks he still loves her.

Because whatever he thinks he feels for her, I'm his person. I'm the person who is easiest to be with. Those were his words.

I don't care if he wants to talk to her. Martin is right: she's bad news. She's bad for Ian. And there's no way I'm going to let her get her hooks into him.

He's mine and I'm going to fight for him.

twenty-four

IAN

I do not know what to do when Savannah leaves me abruptly standing in the kitchen and heads back up the hill to the cottage.

I know what I want to do. I want to go after her and bring her home. Every instinct I have screams at me to do so. I ignore those instincts, because so far today, following my instincts has only made things worse.

I call Martin, but the call rolls immediately to voicemail. Right. He said he was in Dallas meeting with a client this weekend.

I try searching for advice online, but I don't have to tell you how quickly that gets dark. After five minutes down that Internet rabbit hole, I close the window, clear my browser history, and make a sizable donation to a nonprofit focused on date-rape prevention.

Out of options, I call my mom.

She babbles for a good ten minutes about the volunteer work she's been doing at the local library before I interrupt her and tell her I need advice about women.

"Ian, you know I love you, but it's not nice to fuck with me like that."

"What do you mean?"

"You're obviously testing me. After what happened with Ava, you told me that if I ever tried to interfere with your love life again, you'd devote your considerable fortune to changing your identity and moving to another country. Obviously, this is a test. I'm not going to fail it."

"This isn't a test. I've met someone and—"

"If you have met someone, fantastic. I look forward to receiving the wedding invitation. Until then, I'm not falling for it."

"I'm serious, Mom. I'm not testing you."

"Do you remember what you said to me before you threatened to move to another country and change your identity?"

Staring out at the view of the lake, I scrub my hand down my face. "No."

"You said, and I quote, 'No grown man in his thirties wants advice about his sex life from his mother.' End quote."

"Seriously, Mom? For five years, all you could talk about was how you didn't want me to be alone. How you wanted me to find someone who could love me. Someone who would give you grandchildren. And now you're shutting me down?"

"You were very clear about setting boundaries. Yes, I want you to find someone who loves you. I want you to find someone who will give me grandchildren. But I also wanna see those grandchildren when you have them. So I'm staying out of it."

And then she hangs up on me.

If Martin heard the conversation, he would be laughing his ass off right now. Of course, if Martin was around to hear the conversation, I wouldn't have had it with my mother. I'd have just gotten advice from him.

Clearly, I need more friends.

A matter I'm still contemplating, when Mr. Sniggles walks into the kitchen, sits down in front of me, and meows plaintively.

"Do you have any advice?" I ask the cat.

He meows again, then he gives head butts to my

shins before walking over to his food bowl. Okay, so he's hungry. I pour a little dry kibble into the bowl and then dump out a can of food on top.

"She left quickly," I tell the cat. "But we know she's coming back, right? It's not like she would abandon you. Me? Maybe. You? Definitely not. And she's just up the hill in the cottage. I know where she is. So there's no point in panicking, right? I just have to wait for her to come back."

So that's what I do. I pour myself a cup of coffee, open my laptop on the bar, and I wait.

I eat a biscuit. I stare sightlessly at the latest grant proposal. After ten minutes, I give up trying to concentrate on it. I open a new browser window and pull up everything I can find about Savannah, her father, her brother, Blake, and Embarcado.

On my iPad, I make notes on what I could do to rectify the situation. Whatever I do, I'm going to get Martin's input. Which leaves me with more questions than answers for the moment.

Why didn't I look into any of this earlier?

I'm still on the first page of search results when I hear tires on the gravel driveway. I pull up the security camera just in time to see a white SUV park in front of my house. Ava climbs out.

She's in high heels and one of those skin-tight dresses that leaves most of her legs bare. Her hair is loose around her shoulders, her eyes covered in huge sunglasses, and her pursed lips painted scarlet. It's Sunday morning before noon and she looks dressed for a night on the town.

She pushes the doorbell impatiently.

Martin was right. I should've had a gate installed on the road.

She doesn't give me the chance to greet her when I open the door, but sweeps past me into the foyer, saying dramatically, "Please don't send me away. Just hear me out."

I'm enveloped by the scent of a ten thousand dollar an ounce perfume. Yeah, I know that's how much it cost, because she had me foot the bill when she hired a private perfumer to craft a signature scent for her.

For ten thousand dollars an ounce, you would think he could've come up with something I actually liked.

"Ava," I say, by way of greeting. I glance out the door in time to see the driver pulling away. "I hope you didn't tell your driver to leave."

She ignores me as she crosses the living area to stand by the windows looking out at the view of the lake. She sighs, then turns around to lean against the windows and drags her sunglasses off. "Don't pretend you haven't missed me."

"Okay." It hadn't occurred to me to pretend I had any feelings for her one way or another.

"I know how hard the past year has been on you."

"You do?"

She walks over to me with an exaggerated sway in her hips, tossing her sunglasses onto the side table as she does, stopping only a few inches from me, before reaching up to cup my jaw in her hands.

She keeps my jaw in her hands and gazes up at me. "I know I hurt you. We hurt each other."

God, I hate it when she does this shit. When she treats every moment as if it's being filmed. As if this isn't a life, but a carefully scripted scene meant to evoke drama and emotion. To her, I'm not a person. I'm a set piece. A bit of background for her to interact with, that shows her in her best light.

"That's why you've been hiding out here in isolation for a year."

I move to step back away from her touch but realize she's got me backed against the wall.

"I haven't been hiding."

"None of our friends have seen you in months. I thought I would see you at South By, but you weren't there."

"Our friends?" I wasn't really aware we had any friends in common, since she and Martin never got along and she described everyone I worked with as *socially stunted and impossibly dull.*

"Yes, our friends." She rattles off a list of names I barely recognize. A few I vaguely remember as being social media influencers in town. None of them are people I would call friends.

Before I can say as much, she rises on her toes like she's going to kiss me, murmuring, "You poor, poor man."

Backed against the wall or no, she's gotten too close. I cup her shoulders so I can extract myself and order her to leave. Before I can, the front door opens and Savannah bursts in.

I've never been so happy to see someone in my life. She's still dressed in the tank top and overalls she was wearing earlier. Her feet are bare, which suggests she walked all the way down the gravel driveway from the cottage here barefoot. She's out of breath; I can see her chest rising and falling.

She scans the room, her gaze landing on Ava and me. I know exactly how it looks: Ava standing too close, one hand on my jaw, the other on my chest, my hands on her arms, like I'm about to pull her to me.

Even I, who struggle to grasp the subtleties of social interactions, can see that this is a shit show.

SAVANNAH

I run at breakneck speed down the gravel driveway to the main house, desperately wishing I'd actually stopped to put on shoes. Ian said the gravel driveway is great for the environment—something to do with impervious surfaces and the water table —but it's hell on bare feet.

The gleaming white SUV passes me on the way down and I have to jump out of the way to avoid being hit. By the time I reach the main house, I'm even more out of breath than I was when I walked up the hill earlier, as improbable as that seems.

I throw open the door, still scrubbing my feet on the doormat to dislodge the gravel lodged in my soles. The second I look up and see the scene before me, panic sets in for real.

They are obviously in an embrace. He's about to kiss her. When he turns to look at me, jaw tight, brows knitted, I know my interruption has pissed him off.

I flinch back instinctively, my breath still coming in short bursts from my run down the hill.

Fuck.

Should I leave?

What am I doing here, anyway?

He's a grown man who can make his own decisions and who is clearly still in love with his ex.

I should go. Now.

Except ... Ava looks me up and down, a sneer twisting her lips, a spark of cruelty in her gaze.

I don't know if it's that—the way she looks at me like I'm a bug—or if it's the way her scarlet tipped, manicured nails curl like talons on his chest. Whichever it is, no.

Just, no.

I'm not leaving. I'm not backing down.

Maybe he still has feelings for her. Maybe he even still thinks he loves her. I don't care.

She's bad for him.

I trust Martin enough to know that he has Ian's

best interests at heart. I don't trust myself to be objective, but I do trust him.

She will not get her claws into him again. Not on my watch.

Not that I have a plan for forcing her to leave. Or a plan of any kind beyond catching my breath.

Stupid fucking virus!

I sag against the wall by the door, still struggling to pull air into my lungs.

"Who are you?" Ava exclaims.

"Hey!" I try to sound bright and cheerful, like I just stopped by instead of hurtling down the hill to cockblock her. "I just …" I wheeze a little more, then dissolve into a coughing fit.

Before I can recover, Ian strides across the room, catching my arms to help me straighten. "Are you okay? Did you run all the way here?"

He runs his gaze over me, looking for signs of fragility or weakness. Sweet, protective Ian …

And just like that, a plan forms. I just need to distract him long enough to pry him from her grasp. If he thinks I'm about to pass out, that will keep her lips off of him until Martin gets here.

I can do that, right?

And it's only mildly immoral because I'm doing it for his own good.

I lean weakly against the window, pressing my

hand to my chest like I'm struggling for breath. "I'm ... fine. Just give me ..."

Before I can gasp out the end of my sentence, he sweeps me into his arms, bride-style.

My arms go automatically around his neck as he carries me across the room as though I weigh nothing.

He really is quite good at this whole carrying-me-around thing. He could do it professionally. Or win gold in the Olympics.

In the living room, he deposits me on the sectional and kneels by my side, giving me a searing once over, as if searching for injuries. "Do you need me to call Dr. Berry?"

"Who is this person?" Ava demands shrilly. "Is she some sort of farmer?"

I ignore her. Ian's hand is on the center of my chest, carefully gauging the rise and fall of my chest. "Just breathe," he murmurs.

I breathe in deeply, my gaze on his as he draws in air matching his breath to mine. Fake or not, it's soothing being the center of his attention, feeling as though he's coaxing me back from the brink of collapse. As if there really is a bond between us, woven by our solitude and proximity over the past few months. Not to mention the amazing sex of the past couple of days.

Well, sex that was amazing for me. Even if it was only rebound sex for him.

Damn it.

I'm hit with another wave of panic and now my pulse is hammering again and I will not cry, I will not cry. I will not cry.

Not in front of her.

"I'm going to call the doctor," Ian says, starting to stand, but I don't release his hand.

"What is going on?" Ava shrieks again.

"I'm sure I'll be—Oof!"

I don't finish the sentence, because Mr. Sniggles appears out of nowhere to land on my chest. All twenty-eight pounds of him.

"Not now, big guy." Ian scoops him up to deposit him on the floor.

Mr. Sniggles, indignant, jumps onto the coffee table. Being a cat of excellent taste, he takes an immediate dislike to Ava, and arches his back, tail in the air, and hisses at her.

"What is that thing?" She screeches in response, backing away. "Is that a raccoon?"

Ian doesn't bother to look over his shoulder. "He's a Maine Coon." He says it slowly, like he's talking to a toddler. "Not a raccoon."

Apparently, Ian's tone is the last straw, because Ava marches closer to the sofa and looms over Ian, where he's still squatting by my side. "I demand an explanation. Who is this person? Why is she here? Why is this animal in your house?" She sneezes several times—a high-pitched, whole-body spasm that's at odds with her elegant appearance. "You know I'm allergic to cats!"

Ian twists and stands in one smooth motion. "Actually," he says cooly. "I did not know that."

I can't see his expression, only hers as she reacts to his words. Her eyes twitch, like she's trying to either repress a seizure or decide exactly how to play this.

After a long moment, she tries to smile sweetly, but doesn't quite pull it off. "Well, then, can you please put this creature outside so we can continue our conversation?"

I scramble up from the sofa, keeping close enough to Ian that it appears we're providing a united front. "Oh, Mr. Sniggles can't go outside. He's an indoor cat. And there are coyotes."

Ian glances down at me, his lips curving into the faint hint of a smile. "And possibly wolves."

Ava huffs indignantly—or perhaps she's genuinely having trouble breathing. Though, maybe not if her clipped tone is any sign. "I never did hear who you are."

"I'm Savannah." I smile beatifically and thrust out my hand. "I'm his girlfriend."

Ava huffs indignantly. Mr. Sniggles rubs against her calf. Horrified, Ava tries to shoo Mr. Sniggles away with her shoe and all but kicks him.

At which point Ian says, "If you're going to kick our cat, I'll have to ask you to leave."

And just like that, he has his hand at her elbow and he's showing her to the door over protests about her car already being gone and it being too hot outside to wait on the porch.

I don't hear anything after that, because he follows her out onto the porch and shuts the door behind him.

I sit back down on the sofa. Then stand up again. Then pace for a moment.

Should I follow them out?

Should I let them wait for her car alone or do I need to chaperone?

It feels like I ruined the mood and that her kicking Mr. Sniggles was a deal breaker for him, but what if I'm wrong? What if she's out there right now … casting a spell on him? Or whatever glamorous women do to lure men in.

I pace a little more, only to end up in the kitchen, in front of Ian's open laptop. Which has the live feed from the front porch streaming to it.

There's no audio, of course, but I can see her talking quickly. Making her case, no doubt.

I should turn away, but can't seem to make myself. This could be it. The moment the man I really, really like—maybe more than really, really like—dives head first back into a relationship with the woman who broke his heart.

And there's nothing I can do to stop him.

On the screen, I see him hold up a hand as if to cut her off. She snaps her mouth closed. I can't see his face, so I don't know if he's talking, but I assume so, because I see her nodding as she gazes up at him.

Is he telling her I'm not his girlfriend?

Is he explaining that I'm just the hired help?

An uppity employee with a fragile immune system who wriggled her way into his home?

As if he can feel my gaze on him, Ian slowly twists to look directly into the camera. I stumble back a step and slap the laptop closed, only to realize that will just confirm to him I was spying on him.

Oh, for the love of butter.

I pace the kitchen a bit, then realize there are still biscuits sitting out on the pan. So I grab one, split it in half, load it up with butter, and shove half a biscuit into my mouth.

And that's when I hear the front door open and

then close. I whirl around to see him standing at the front door. He pins me with a look as he crosses to the kitchen. Meanwhile, I'm still struggling to produce enough saliva to swallow without choking.

He looks from me to the butter knife in my hand and I imagine he can see every golden brown, delicious biscuit crumb dotting my overalls.

"Mmmbsorby."

Um ... yeah.

If I could have a do over on today, I would definitely wear something more glamorous than overalls. Of course, I did not know that I would be face to face with an actual Hollywood starlet. Homegirl may be a bitch, but she is even more beautiful in person than she is on the screen.

And here I am, unable to even talk past the food in my mouth.

I wipe at my mouth with the back of my hand, swallow, swallow again, grab the nearest coffee cup and choke down a gulp of cold coffee and try again. "I'm sorry."

Ian tips his head to the side. "For what?"

"For lying to Ava. About being your girlfriend."

Ian's frown deepens.

Almost against my will, I keep talking, babbling in a geyser of nerves. "Martin called and said Ava was on her way over. He said she's bad news and you shouldn't be alone with her. So I ran down here. But she was about to kiss you. So I did the only thing I could think of to distract you."

He seems to be puzzling through my admission. "So you pretended to be ill?"

"Yes… I mean, sort of, I guess? I was winded after running down the hill. But mostly I was trying to distract you. And it worked. And then I told her I was your girlfriend because I thought it would make her leave. And it did. And now … we're here."

Fantastic.

I am a brilliant orator. I should obviously run for office. Or maybe offer to write for Rachel Maddow. My ability to sum up complex situations is top-notch.

Ian takes a step closer, still looking confused. "What were you apologizing for again?"

"For lying to Ava about being your girlfriend."

Suddenly, he seems very close.

"Was that a lie?" He reaches up to brush more crumbs away with his thumb.

"I …"

Oh god. I can't think.

Not when he's this close, and he's touching me.

Or maybe I have brain damage from being so out of breath. That's believable, right?

"Is it *not* a lie?" I ask. When he doesn't respond, I

swallow, muster my courage and ask more point-edly, "Am I your girlfriend?"

His gaze pauses in its perusal of my face. "I understand some linguists object to the term on the grounds that it infantilizes women."

"Is that your objection to the term?"

"No." He steps closer, reaching up to cup my jaw. "I object to the term because it feels temporary. Impermanent."

"Oh."

Whatever else I was going to say gets lost as he lowers his mouth to mine in a kiss that's sweet and simple and hints at just enough more that I find myself once again breathless.

Wanting this moment to last more than I should, I push against his shoulders and he immedi-ately raises his head.

"Wait. What about Ava?"

"What about her?"

"She was just here. You were about to kiss her not ten minutes ago." God. I can't believe I'm saying this. "And she wants you back."

He stiffens. "What? Is that what that was about?"

Oh, this daft, daft man.

"Did you not get that?"

"I ..." He tips his head to the side again. "She kept

talking about how lonely she thought I was. And how sorry she was that she hurt me. She didn't mention getting back together."

Oh, dear.

Don't spell it out for him! part of me screams.

If she didn't know enough about how to communicate with him to get straight to the point, then she doesn't deserve him!

On the other hand, he needs to know. If she's the one he wants, if he picks her over me, then he doesn't deserve me.

I blow out a breath. "She came here—looking like that—because she wants you back. I don't know if it took her that long to realize how stupid she was to let you go or what, but that's why she was here. And —" God, this part is going to kill me. "—If you really love her, this is your chance."

Here I am, holding my breath, waiting to hear his response, and Ian just keeps staring at me.

After a moment, he says, "Okay."

And then he leans down to kiss me again.

I shove my hands between us. "Okay? That's all you're going to say?"

"What else should I say?"

"I don't know. Something more than just okay! You were in love with her! She broke your heart! And now she wants you back, so I think that warrants more than just an okay."

"Wait. Do you want me to get back together with her?"

"No. God, no! I just ... you were in love with her and—"

He steps away, hands propped on his hips. "Why do you keep saying that?"

"What?"

"That I was in love with her." He scrubs a hand down his face. "I wasn't."

"But..." I study him, trying to filter through all the things he's said and done that led me to that conclusion. "After she left, you sold your company and moved out here to the lake. You became a recluse."

"I stepped down as CEO of Cookie Jar long before I started dating her. Taking the company public was in the works for years. Ava would never have dated me if I hadn't had all that IPO cash. I didn't move out here to the lake because I was brokenhearted. I moved out here because being with her made me realize how disgusted I was by my life in Austin."

"Oh."

"The six months I dated her were the worst of my life. She wanted me to travel with her, all the time. It was endless parties with people I didn't know and movie premieres for shit I didn't want to see. The only thing she ever cared about was spending my money and how we looked together in pictures."

"Then why did you stay with her for six months?" It's a rude question, but one I can't help but ask.

"I don't know. Everyone I knew kept telling me it was supposed to be fun. That I'd worked so hard all my life and that this was supposed to be my reward. Here I was, dating this woman that everyone told me was gorgeous and amazing, at parties where everyone else seemed to have the time of their lives. I was bored to tears, wearing uncomfortable clothes that I hated, and it was—"

His expression says it all.

I think about how careful he is with his surroundings now. How quiet and peaceful he keeps the house. How all the surfaces are either cold and smooth or silky soft. I've felt his clothes ... Hell, I've worn his clothes. They're all natural fabrics. Nary an itchy tag to be found.

He hasn't said it, but I'm pretty sure he's on the spectrum and that he has sensory processing issues.

Being with Ava—at loud parties, in uncomfortable clothes, surrounded by music and conversation that held no interest for him—it must have been torture.

I want to pull him into my arms and hold him. To shelter him from ever having to face her again.

Instead, I make one final protest. "But you went to therapy for her."

Maybe it's narrow minded of me to think men who go to therapy are extraordinary, since it's the twenty-first century. But this is still Texas and we haven't yet shaken off the stereotype that men are too strong for that kind of nonsense.

But Ian just meets my gaze, his lips twitching, like he's in on the joke. "I went to therapy for me. To figure out why I stayed with her so long. Not because I wanted her back, but because I thought the fact that I'd never wanted her at all meant there was something wrong with me."

And just like that, all my questions and doubts fade away.

Because how could this man, this kind, complicated, beautiful man ever feel like there was something wrong with him?

I pull him back to me, cupping his jaw and steering his gaze to mine. "There is nothing wrong with you. You are perfect."

There's that lip twitch again.

"I am far from perfect." His hand slips up to

mine. He pulls it from his jaw and presses a kiss to my palm. "I am cranky and solitary. I would always rather be at home, where I'm comfortable, with a decent internet connection or a good book than out in the real world with other people. Therapy didn't help me get over Ava. I was never involved with her enough for that. It helped me realize I was okay alone. And I thought that was how I'd live my life from here on out. Alone in my house. In this huge empty house that wasn't even a home before you. It was just a building that I lived in.

"Then you came along. And you are the only person who could have coaxed me out of my shell. The only person I'd want to be with, because being with you feels as natural as breathing. It's like being alone, only better. But I only want that if you want that, too."

I swallow past the tears rising in my eyes as I nod. "Yeah. I think I do want that."

"You kept saying that I loved Ava, but I didn't. I never felt that way about her. I don't think I even knew what love was until you."

My breath catches in surprise. "Love?"

He pulls back, just a little. Like my question startled him. After a minute, he gives one of those decisive nods of his. "Yeah. Love. I love you, Savannah.

He's so close, practically whispering the words

into my skin. I want him. I want his lips on mine. His skin against mine. His heart beating under my palm.

But I also don't want any of those things to happen. I want this moment to have the space it needs. I want to stretch it out, to distort time and space so this moment lasts forever.

I don't know how to respond, how to crack open my heart and show this amazing man all the things he makes me feel. How all his edges match up to mine to fill in the empty places in my heart.

Or maybe I can't find the words because there simply aren't any.

Instead, I turn his hand to brush a kiss on his knuckles. "So, if you don't like the term girlfriend, is there a different term you do like? I'm open to ideas."

His eyes flutter closed, and he presses his forehead briefly to mine. "How about mine?"

SAVANNAH

I stand in the closet, still wrapped in my towel, and stare at the row of clothes while I debate what to wear to meet Trinity and Martin for lunch.

Ian's closet—now our closet—is no longer so empty. It's still too big, even with all of my clothes added in, but it no longer feels lonely.

Maybe it's Mr. Sniggles's cat tree, which Ian built, in the center of the room, complete with a hammock where our beast of a cat is now sleeping. Or maybe it's the way our clothes hang side-by-side seamlessly mixed together, much in the same way our lives are now intertwined.

I get lost staring at the closet and thinking about

how much my life has changed since last summer. I almost don't hear Ian walking up behind me.

I squeal when he wraps his arms around me, nearly picking me up off my feet as he burrows his face into my neck.

"I thought you said we were in a hurry."

"We are."

"Then why are you just standing here, tempting me?"

I laugh, reaching up to thread my fingers through his hair. Is it wrong how much I love it when he's greedy with my time?

We're meeting Martin and Trinity in town for lunch to hash out the details about our destination wedding.

"We can't be late. You know what those two are like."

"Like oil and water," Ian agrees, nodding.

I feel the gesture against my neck where he's still kissing me. Instinctively, I rock my hips back and feel the length of his hard cock against my ass.

"If we're late and they're left alone at the restaurant together, they might burn the damn place down." My words come out breathy, and I'm still rubbing my ass against his cock. "On the other hand, how much damage could they really do?" I turn in his arms, pressing my hands to his bare chest. "If we're only five or ten minutes later."

Probably a lot. It's an open secret that Martin and Trinity don't get along, though neither will explain why.

Ian pulls me even closer, spinning us both so he can back me up against the wall. His mouth moves over mine, stirring the heat low in my belly and making my pussy ache. I loop the fingers of one hand through his belt loops while I press my left palm to his chest, just over his tattoo.

Last month he got his first tattoo, two concentric circles right over his heart. When I rest my hand on his heart, our tattoos line up. Almost the second my hand touches his skin, the energy in the room shifts. The heat that underlies our interaction shifts into something more emotional.

He slides his hands up to cup my jaw, murmuring against my lips, "You hold my heart in the palm of your hand. As always."

"It's a good heart," I murmur back.

"Is it?"

His question surprises me so much I pull back to study his face. That is not how the exchange between us usually goes. "What do you mean? Why would you ask that?"

He ducks his head, averting his gaze. "It's about Blake."

"What?" I would stumble back a step, but my back is already at the wall. "What about him?"

"I've been doing research about him."

"You have? Why?"

Ian's gaze goes hard and narrow as he drops his hands from me and takes a step back. "He hurt you. He stole Embarcado from you."

"Yeah," I say cautiously.

"There should be consequences for that kind of behavior. I could ..." he stumbles over the next words. "...provide those consequences."

"Ian, what did you do?"

"Nothing. Not yet. Martin said I should ask you first, to see what you wanted me to do."

I release a startled burst of laughter. "Yeah, Martin was right. You can't just ... what exactly were you going to do to him?"

Ian slides his hands into his pockets. "He shouldn't have been rewarded for what he did. He shouldn't just get to live his life with wealth and privilege. I happen to have the means to guarantee that his wealth does not last long."

My eyebrows shoot up and I prop my hands on my hips, the towel wiggling precariously as I do. "You're offering to do what here? Bankrupt him?"

Ian's gaze dips and skitters away. "It's hardly fair for us to be having this conversation when you're dressed only in a towel."

"You started this conversation when I was dressed only in a towel. Right after kissing me senseless."

His cheeks flush as he rakes his fingers through his hair. "Yeah well, I thought you were distracted and wouldn't pay this much attention."

I laugh again, this time a genuine laugh. "So you purposefully distracted me while telling me you'd planned to bankrupt my half-brother for revenge?"

He just scowls.

I laugh even more. "You had to know I wasn't going to agree to that."

"You might have," he grumbles. "If I'd found a better way to ask."

I quirk an eyebrow, walking past Ian to go further into the closet and pick out a dress. For real this time. "I don't want revenge."

"But—"

I pull a dress off a hanger and step into it. "I really don't. Look at my life now. I have everything I need." And it's not just Ian, though he alone would be more than enough. Martin has been drawing up papers for me to start my own restaurant. Yes, I'll have some financial backing from Ian, but from other places, too. Friends from the restaurant world who I didn't even know I could count on. "My life is good. Beyond good. Beyond anything I ever could have imagined."

I turn back to Ian, cupping his jaw in my hands to meet his gaze, getting lost for a moment in his eyes. His amazing, soulful eyes that look at me like I'm his whole universe.

I want so desperately for him to understand what he means to me. And how little I need the revenge he's offering.

"I appreciate that you want to do something to make this right, but I don't need it. Honestly. I have you. You are all I need. Besides, Blake had a family who loved him and he gave it up for money. Whatever comes his way in life, he's getting what he deserves." I pull a shirt off a hanger for Ian and hand it to him. "Now get yourself dressed."

He takes the shirt from me, head cocked to the side like he's thinking. "So just to be clear, you don't want me to bankrupt Blake?"

"Correct. I expressly forbid you from messing with his finances at all."

After a long moment, Ian nods, sliding his arms into his shirt and starting on the buttons. His fingers are slow, like he's still deep in thought, so I brush them aside and take over the job for him, pausing only long enough to press my tattoo to his.

"It is a good heart. And an amazing life."

texts between savannah and trinity

ONE YEAR LATER

OMG. Have you seen this???

What? Seen what?

THIS

<link to news article>

LOVE AFFAIR BETWEEN DISGRACED MOVIE STARLETTE AVA GRAYSON AND FAILED RESTAURATEUR BLAKE LEWIS COMES TO DRAMATIC END AMID ALLEGATIONS OF CHEATING, DRUG USE, AND PETTY CRIMES

Crazy, right?

OMG

RIGHT?

OMG!!!!!

RIGHT???

It says they were introduced by a mutual friend a few months ago.

I didn't even know they were dating. Did you?

No. I didn't.

Apparently, they were hot and heavy for a while and then

And I quote

"They're relationship spiraled quickly out of control."

So bizarre, right?

You have no idea

texts between ian
and savannah

What did you do?

What?

<link to news article>

LOVE AFFAIR BETWEEN
DISGRACED MOVIE STARLETTE
AVA GRAYSON AND FAILED
RESTAURATEUR BLAKE LEWIS
COMES TO DRAMATIC END AMID
ALLEGATIONS OF CHEATING,
DRUG USE, AND PETTY CRIMES

Was this you?

I don't know what you mean.

Did you make that happen?

I don't see how you think I could
have made that happen.

Did you introduce them or something?

You forbid me from messing with Blake's finances

Therefore I have not messed with his finances

Did you do something else?

You said Blake would get what he deserved.

I believe that he did.

And that Ava did as well.

Don't think I haven't noticed that you're refusing to answer whether or not you had *anything* to do with it.

IAN HAS SILENCED NOTIFICATIONS

Welp, I guess that's my answer.

I love you, you silly, ridiculous, over-protective man.

As always, you hold my heart in your hand.

I hope you enjoyed reading Ian and Savannah's story as much as I enjoyed writing it. If you did, please consider leaving me a review. a review. Hey, even if you didn't! Reviews are universally awesome and appreciated!

Also … keep reading if you want a glimpse of Martin and Trinity's book, Pretense & Sensibility.

Join my newsletter for bonus epilogues, deleted scenes and a FREE BOOK. Just follow the QR Code...

<u>**Emma Lee Jayne**</u>

I write the kinds of books I want to read. Fast-paced books with lots of world-building, snarky heroines, and swoony heroes. I love story, pop culture, gossip, and baked goods. I'm a modern-day hippy and certified LEGO nerd.

I live in the Austin, Texas hill country, with my geeky husband and two extremely geeky kids. We have dogs, chickens, cats, and more LEGOs than should be allowed by law.

www.emmaleejayne.com

pretense &
sensibility

Martin

One year ago

I've had a long day, even before I get a call from my grandmother's doctor reminding me that I've missed the last three appointments to discuss her care. She's in a top-notch memory care center. I pay good money and lots of it so that I don't have to drop everything every time she needs any little thing. But the doctors definitely know how to lay on the guilt.

So after a grueling day, I drive across town to the Precious Meadows Care Center where I am verbally whipped by every employee who knows me by sight. Yes, I've missed appointments. Yes, I know I don't visit as often as I should. Yes, I feel like a horrible grandson.

Hey, I put in serious effort the first three years she was here, but the less she knows me, the harder it is to come visit. So I don't.

By the time I make it back to my mother's room, all I want to do is say a quick hello, confirm what I already know—she won't recognize or remember me—and then get out.

Five minutes, tops, in and out.

I know my hopes were misplaced the second I enter the private room and see the woman there with her.

It's the woman from the lobby—Hot Mess Princess Leia.

I have no idea who she is, but that's how I've been thinking of her ever since I saw her. Not that I've been thinking about her.

But she did make quite an impression.

She is, to use her own words, a hot mess.

She's younger than my thirty years by at least a decade. She's dressed in baggy cargo pants and a T-shirt that reads "May the flock be with you." The shirt is worn and just tight enough to show off an amazing pair of tits. Which makes me genuinely sad I'm too tired to appreciate them.

She's a little taller than average for a woman, but there is a delicacy to her frame and her heart-shaped face that gives the impression she's fragile. Her hair is brown and up in two messy buns on either side of her head, just like Princess Leia.

Which is even weirder, since she yelped the words "Princess Leia," when she fell on her ass.

If I wasn't so damn tired, or in a better mood, and didn't feel like I had been tortured all morning, the incident in the lobby probably would've been amusing. I might have even noticed how undeniably attractive the woman is.

But today being what it is, I put her out of my mind until I walked into my grandmother's room and found her there.

"Who are you precisely?"

She seems to have trouble understanding my question, looking for me to my grandmother and back again over and over like she's stuck in a time loop.

She frowns and gives her head a little shake. "This can't..." she mutters before trailing off.

"Are you some kind of a candy striper?"

Do they even have those anymore? Did they ever have those or was that just something you saw on TV shows?

"No, I'm not a candy striper!" she blurts.

"Some kind of nurse's aid?" I ask, since she was clearly offended by the suggestion that she's a candy striper. She's way too young to be a doctor. "Maybe a volunteer?"

She's still frowning. Still wearing that stunned and confused expression. Which is when a horrible thought occurs to me. Precious Meadows specializes in caring for Alzheimer's patients, but not exclusively. Some of their residents are younger people who aren't able to care for themselves. Given her obvious confusion ...

Fuck.

No wonder she looks so distressed by my presence.

I'm not a small guy. And I have it on good authority that I'm a grumpy asshole even when I'm not physically and emotionally exhausted.

I uncross my arms and let my hands drop to my sides, purposefully letting my shoulders drop so that I look a little less scary. Then I say, in my most gentle, soothing voice, "You look worried. Can I help you with anything? Do you need someone to take you back to your room?"

"My ... what?" Her features pinch in confusion before settling into a glare of indignation. "I don't have room here. I'm not a resident."

Which might well be what she would say if she was.

"Okay," I hold out my hands, palms out. "No worries. Let me just get one of the aids."

But before I can even take a step back towards the door, Hot Mess Princess Leia marches over to me and pokes me in the chest with her finger.

"I am not a resident." She punctuates each word with a jab. "I am a close, personal friend of Margaret's."

"That's interesting," I say with what I hope is diplomacy. "Because you're what? Twenty? Twenty-one? And you're close personal friends with a woman in her seventies?"

"I am a family friend!"

Her ferocity would almost be cute if I wasn't starting to think this woman might actually be delusions. And if her fingers weren't so pokey.

She jabs me again. "And I'll have you know that I am twenty-three."

I grab her hand before she can jab me again. "Please stop that." My voice is no longer gentle and soothing. Maybe because this woman is really starting to piss me off. Maybe because her finger is pointier that it looks. Maybe because I've found myself holding her hand in mine, standing far closer to her than I should, when I haven't touched a woman—at least not sexually—in ... fuck, it's probably been at least a year.

All of that combines to create a surge of emotion that I hardly have the capacity to unpack. More than a little irritation, a fuck-ton of frustration, and a solid dose of physical attraction.

I absolutely don't have time for this and she's probably too young for me. And it doesn't matter how old she is, because ... Have I mentioned that I don't have time for this?

My best friend and most important client is in the middle of having his life implode. So no, I don't have the time or bandwidth to be attracted to a stranger right now.

Even one who's looking at me with the widest, brightest blue eyes I think I've ever seen. Even one who smells like cinnamon and vanilla and fresh baked cookies.

I don't have time for this, but damn it, I almost wish I did.

I'm about to drop her hand and put some distance between us—I swear I'm about to—when I hear the unexpected sound of—

"Is that a chicken?" I ask.

"Oh." The woman pulls her hand from mine and takes a jerking step backwards. "Oh!" she exclaims a second time, looking frantically around the room. "Oh, Princess Leia! I completely forgot about her!"

"Princess Leia?" I repeat, because everything about this afternoon has taken a turn for the bizarre. I look around the room half expecting someone else in Star Wars themed clothing to pop out of no where.

Instead of answering me, Hot Mess Princess Leia drops to her hands and knees and makes to crawl under the bed. Perfect round ass up in the air, she wiggles her torso under the bed while murmuring, "It's okay, sweetie. Just give me a second and I'll get you... Ow! Damn it! I'm trying to help... Stop that!"

All the while a series of clucks and squawks emanate from under the bed. Punctuated with more exclamations of pain, from both the woman and the bird, if I was to guess.

Then the squawks increase, the muttering morphs into the soothing murmuring and her butt starts to wiggle out from under the bed. A moment later she stands up. One of the hair knots is lopsided, the other is gone completely. Her shirt is crooked and her bare arms covered in red peck marks. And she's holding a small chicken, covered in ridiculous orange fluff in the crook of her arm.

"Princess Leia?" I ask.

The woman tips her head in confusion as she strokes the bird with her closed fist, literally smoothing it's ruffled feathers. "No. Princess Lay-a." She says this like it should have been obvious to me. As though there should have been no room for confusion, despite the Star Wars themed T-shirt and the buns on the top of her head. "Like how player becomes playa. Layer, lay-a. As in she lays eggs."

As she says the word eggs, she hold out her fisted hand and opens it to reveal a small egg. I take it automatically. It's still warm.

Apparently, that's what all the clucking was about just now.

The chicken makes another agitated squawk. My grandmother chooses that moment to say, "Oh, is Princess Lay-a here?"

The woman arches an eyebrow, as if the question proves some kind of a point. Then she marches over to my grandmother, chicken still in her arms.

"Yes, but she and I were just about to leave. Can you hold her for me while I pack up?"

My grandmother takes the chicken and holds her close to her chest, gentle stroking the birds feathers. Her expression is serene as she coos to the bird. The woman looks decidedly less serene as she packs up a collection of things scattered around the room. A large photo album I don't recognize, an iPad and phone all get shoved into a backpack dotted with Millennium Falcons, that's then slung over her delicate shoulders. Finally she opens the soft-sided pet carrier.

Only when she moves to my grandmother's side do her movements gentle. She extracts the bird from my grandmother's grasp, murmuring something barely louder than the chicken's coos. Then, she zips the bird into the pet carrier and marches out.

The door gives it's familiar buzz to alert the staff at the station that someone is leaving the room. As I watch the woman walk away, I see one of the orderlies wave at her. Hot Mess Princess Leia is not a resident--obviously. Which means she must be someone who either works or volunteers here.

Once she rounds the corner and leaves my sight, I look back at my mom. "Who the hell was that?"

"Language, Marty. Please."

For a moment, my grandmother looks so much like her former self, it just about kills me.

I clear my throat. "Okay. Who was that woman?"

"That was Trinity. She's new here." Then she tips her head to the side and adds, "You know, I've always thought you and Trinity would be perfect together."

I don't know whether to laugh or cry. Or punch something.

Actually, yeah. Punching something would feel really good about now. Maybe I'd even do it, except I'm still holding the damn egg.

Pre-order now!